Galisteo

NIGHTS

Galisteo

NIGHTS

KELLI LEE MISTRY

ASA PUBLISHING CORPORATION
AN INNOVATIVE OUTSOURCE BOOK PUBLISHING HYBRID

1285 N. Telegraph Rd., #376, Monroe, Michigan 48162
An Accredited Publishing House with the Better Business Bureau
www.asapublishingcorporation.com

Copyrights©2020, Kelli Lee Mistry, All Rights Reserved
Book Title: Galisteo Nights
Date Published: 04.11.2020
Book ID: ASAPCID2380739
Edition: 1 *Trade Paperback*
ISBN: 978-1-946746-69-6
Library of Congress Cataloging-in-Publication Data

BBB
100 YEARS
Advancing Trust Together

This book was published in the United States of America.
Great State of Michigan

Table of Contents

INTRODUCTION

Do you believe in love? Do you believe in spirits? If you do, you will get wrapped up in this love story between a ghost and a man. There is even a love triangle to make it more interesting. It is set in the South West, in New Mexico, a very ancient and mysterious place in a town that is off the beaten path. The characters in this story are full of depth and complexities; they will make you laugh and make you cry. Most of all, they will steal your heart.

I hope you enjoy this story,

Kelli Lee Mistry

Galisteo
NIGHTS

KELLI LEE MISTRY

CHAPTER ONE

I lie gazing upon the stars with my love, Anna; it feels as if we are connected by heartstrings. I feel blessed to have her in my life, truly blessed. She snuggles closer to me; together, we fit like two puzzle pieces made for one another. It is hard to believe that we have only been livin' together for just over a year now; I cannot imagine life without her—before or after this moment. I savor occasions like this, which is just one moment in time but a memory that will live vividly within my heart for years to come. She brings me back to the present with a gentle reminder that I have to be up early to tend the cattle and horses on the ranch; after all, they are the reason we are blessed to be livin' here on this vast high desert plane, underneath the beautiful stars of Galisteo, New Mexico.

I worked on this ranch when I was a youngster, really, only

about 16 years old; it was just a temporary position while I was in high school. I later earned a scholarship to college out East for football. I was good lookin', lithe, and fast as an athlete. I was coveted as a cornerback by many schools, yet, I chose Yale, for it seemed prestigious, and I thought the Ivy League education would be respected by my peers. I was rakishly handsome and thought I would date a cheerleader, marry, and have an NFL-pro career. Sometimes God has different plans.

When we are young, it seems that our dreams are endless; we believe that they will all come true. Sadly, mine evaporated when I was injured durin' my junior year, thus, ending my football career. Academically I was an average student; all of my energy was put into my athletic career, thus, leaving little time left for studies. I fell into a deep depression after the injury and became addicted to pain pills. I decided to drop out of college—in hindsight, maybe a poor decision. Dreams die hard. I don't regret my past choices, for they brought me here to live in this idyllic place with her.

We headed to the house and our bed; I cherished the feel of Anna's body against mine. Chills raced over my skin, where she stroked me ever so lightly as we entered that dream state. Every night I would have vivid dreams with Anna as the star. We would be lyin' on a blanket up on the ridge overlookin' the ranch. Our picnic items were scattered about as we languidly basked in the afterglow of our lovemakin'. She loved being outside when we made love. She always tells me, "There is nothing better than doing what comes naturally in nature." I had to agree. Other times we were in the house. Every night she brought me to ecstasy no matter the backdrop.

The sunbeams felt warm on my skin as they danced around the room, awakenin' me from my reverie. I almost hated to see the mornin' come as the nights were so special. But come it must the and there are many responsibilities to tend to out here on this three-thousand-acre spread, what with the outbuildings and the sprawlin' adobe style ranch house, I was always repairin' something when I wasn't tendin' to the critters.

I began the chores by feedin' the horses as I needed to saddle up Chase and head to the backcountry, where I would check on the fences and cattle. I loved Chase as he was a beautiful black geldin' and as solid as and steady as they come. He is well suited for ranch work. I went back to the house to get my fuel for the day, strong black coffee, and a heap of food. Anna did not cook, so I had a housekeeper come in six days a week. Sadie certainly knew her way around a kitchen, and I felt blessed to have her, especially since she spoils us.

Anna was waiting at the table. She said she had eaten prior to my coming in. She gazed at me as I consumed my meal. I never tired of her eyes upon me; they were deep pools of blue as endless as the sky.

She said my name quietly, "Seth."

I answered her with an inquisitive look.

She added, "I would like to come with you today. Can you saddle up Jorge for me?"

"Sure thing, beautiful, he will be ready and waitin' in the barn."

Anna loved the sorrel horse named George, although she insisted on calling him Jorge for whatever reason, she wouldn't say.

I finished up and thanked Sadie for her amazin' culinary treats and headed to the barn. It was always a pleasure to be around the horses. The smell of the barn, the hay, horse sweat, even the manure was heavenly to my senses. The only thing that smelled better was Anna; her scent was like night jasmine in bloom. Back to the task at hand—saddlin' horses.

George and Chase, born only one month apart, were raised together, and they were the best of friends. They seemed to enjoy goin' out together, and it was a good thing they were close since Anna would not take the reins. She always made me pony, Jorge. Even though it was a bit of a hindrance to my work, I didn't mind though as long as she was happy.

Sadie had packed a picnic lunch for us, and we headed out to the north ridge, where the cattle liked to spend most of their time. When we arrived, I saw a calf with his leg caught in the barbed wire. It took a bit of doin,' but I was able to cut him free and repair the fence. He got off easy as there were only a few scratches on his legs. I went to the saddlebag and took out the bag balm ointment and rubbed it on the little guy's wounds. He was not happy about being restrained after his ordeal, but all was forgotten when he returned to his mama and began to suckle.

Anna was sitting on a large boulder in the shade, "Sure is a hot one today, Seth."

I agreed as sweat trickled down my brow. I took out my bandana and wiped it away. I went over to Anna with the canteen and sat down beside her. I offered her a sip, but she declined, saying she just had a drink while I was working, and I was the one who needed to stay hydrated. I took a swig and felt the cool liquid soothe my parched throat, grateful for the reprieve from the grueling sun.

Another three hours passed. The fences on the north ridge and the western border were checked, and we decided to eat our lunch. Sadie went above and beyond as always. Bean salad, cornbread, pulled pork, and iced sweet tea. She even had some of her famous brownies for a treat. Sadie's husband is a lucky man.

I gobbled my food, yet Anna barely touched hers. Before I could inquire why, there was a ruckus, and one of the horses broke loose from where he was tied. I went over to steady him and then retied him. I could not see what had caused the horse to break free, but it must have been a snake or bee, somethin' sure startled him. After gettin' him back where he belonged, I came over to Anna and kissed her on her forehead. I whispered in her ear, "Lil' Missy, we have to get back to work, or we will be out here 'til the mornin'."

Off we went, her bein' led by me and life couldn't be better! The rest of the day was uneventful; I repaired a few broken areas of the fence and checked the round bales and water troughs, and we headed back to the barn. A chill was settin' in, and I was lookin' forward to a hot bath and a fire in the fireplace as we settled in for the evenin'. That is the one thing about the desert; the temps are extreme and forever changin'.

After the bath, Anna asked, "Can you read to me from my favorite book of poetry?"

"I would be much obliged," I replied and proceeded to do so. She loves Elizabeth Bishop's work; her poetry forces us to discover the hidden places in everyday moments, and the places where real meaning and big questions lurk. Another favorite of hers is *What the Living Do*, by Marie Howe, but tonight she wanted to hear Elizabeth:

"I said to myself" three days and you'll be seven years old. I was saying it to stop the sensation of falling off the round, turning world into cold, blue-black space. But I felt: you are an I, you are an Elizabeth, you are one of the . . ."

I loved watchin' her face as I read this passage; her eyes

were full of light as she took in every word, she seemed to never tire of hearing it.

I looked over and Anna had dozed off lyin' on the sheepskin rug, I decided to let her sleep by the fire. I tucked her in with a warm cozy blanket, kissed her on the cheek, and snuck up to bed.

I missed her, yet once I drifted into that other realm, the dreams came as vivid as ever. Me lyin' on the ground with Anna on top of me with her sweet caress and gentle motion as she rocked back and forth astride me. Rockin' until I felt I would explode . . . pure bliss. Morning came again as it always does, rudely pullin' me from my pleasure.

Anna was in the kitchen with Sadie. Although I have never heard them speak to one another, they seemed comfortable just bein' in one another's company. I started out with pleasantries for both. "How did you sleep?" I teased Anna. "I missed you in the bed, sleepyhead."

Anna replied, "I slept well."

I asked Sadie, "How was your evenin', and, more importantly, what is for breakfast?"

Sadie teased, "I will not bother answering the first question as I know you are only interested in the second. Pancakes, grits, and bacon," were all she listed.

I helped myself to a cup of coffee and sat beside my girl.

Today I needed to drive into Santa Fe and pick up some parts for the tractor as it has been runnin' a bit rough lately. I asked Anna, "Would you like to tag along?"

She answered, "No, I want to do a bit of reading, and I am not feeling up to a long drive today."

"Okay then ladies, I will see you later this afternoon, have a beautiful day."

Sadie looked at me oddly and replied, "Bye, boss."

I hopped into the pickup truck after my chores were done and began the long journey down the dirt access road. I eventually hit Highway 14, the famous Turquoise Trail. I loved this stretch of highway connecting Albuquerque and Santa Fe, with the towns of Golden, Madrid, Galisteo, and Cerrillos in between. Every now and again, I liked to go into Madrid—not much of a town, but yet it was nice to get off the ranch every now and then, and paint the town so to speak. There is live music on the weekend nights and on Sunday afternoons at the Mineshaft, a local hang out and tavern. One of the regulars there is always dressed like an Old West sheriff, the tourists love him!

As I drove to Santa Fe, I contemplated the way I had met Anna and how havin' her in my life has changed me. I remember it like it was yesterday: I was out ridin' fences lookin' for any sections that needed mendin', and I saw her sittin' on a boulder up on the north ridge starin' out over the acreage as if she was in deep thought, perhaps meditatin'.

Approaching her, I asked her what she was doin' on the ranch; her reply was touchin'. She told me that she had grown up near here and that her father worked on the ranch. She had such fond memories of her time here. She told me about playin' with another little girl whose father was a cowhand on the ranch, and she liked to come here and reminisce. For her, this was a place of peace, and she felt rejuvenated after visitin'.

After that day, I would see her regularly in the same area, sittin' there lookin' so peaceful with the sun glintin' off her golden hair like spun honey. We began spendin' more and more time together until I asked her if she would like to live with me. This is a huge place and I have been living here alone, the sole caretaker. "There is plenty of room for two," I told her. She seemed to jump at the chance. I always wonder if it is me or the place that made her so eager to stay.

I arrived at the tractor supply depot. I turned off the engine in my pickup and sauntered inside. "Hey, Jerry," I greeted the man behind the counter, "I got a call that my tractor parts are in."

"Sure thing, Seth, I will have them out to ya' in a jiffy." Jerry returned within a few minutes just as he promised with the parts in tow.

I thanked him. As he turned to walk away, and inquired, "Say, Jerry, do you know anything about the ole' Ames place that I am takin' care of?"

Jerry thought a moment, "Not really, Seth, probably 'bout as much as you know; there was a tragedy and old man Ames spun off into a depression and let things go to rot. The cowhands quit when he wouldn't pay them, and the place was about in shambles. The bank finally took possession of it when the note was not being paid. I hear old man Ames has been institutionalized. That's about all I know, and that is common knowledge."

I thanked him again and walked out to my truck. I decided to have a bite to eat and go to the library. I stopped at Sonic, a treat for me. I loved the cherry limeade, although it cannot hold a candle to Sadie's cookin'.

Later I wandered over to the public library and asked to look at archived microfiche from the newspaper, *The Santa Fe Reporter*. As an afterthought, I looked up a few issues of the *Santa Fe New Mexican*. Just as Jerry said there wasn't much printed about the Ames' place, just a few articles statin' an iconic ranch was comin' to an end. The newspaper reported there was a tragedy involvin' Silas's daughter, although the article gave no specifics. I recall there were a couple little girls runnin' around when I hired on back in high school. One must have been the daughter, as I remember she was about six or seven back then. I am now in my early thirties, so that would make her about twenty-six or so. I will have to look into it more on my next trip into Santa Fe.

As for now, I best be gettin' back to the ranch. The chores

and the cattle never take a vacation on a workin' ranch. Even though this one is just semi-workin', it is workin' none the less.

My cell phone rang just as I pulled onto Highway 14; it was Anna. "I wondered when you are coming home as you are later than usual when you go into Santa Fe."

"On my way, just got gabbin' with Jerry a bit; see ya' soon hun'." I hung up and noted the cell phone was full of static. I could barely hear her; it always seemed to be that way when Anna called me. Must be the distance from the towers to the ranch causin' a bad connection.

I thought to myself how lucky I was to be the one who was hired as the caretaker for the ranch. I seemed to be the only one in the area with a connection to it and the availability to do so. I am thankful the bank approached me, especially as I was in need of a job and a place to stay. Not too many job opportunities for an injured cornerback with half a useless degree, even if it was from a prestigious college. "Once a Bulldog, Always a Bulldog" was the team motto, and that is just what I feel like; I'm stuck for eternity as a Yale Bulldog, but now I am a stray Bulldog. I need to get out of the past and move on.

Anna ran out to meet me as soon as I pulled into the driveway. She seemed so happy I was home. I asked about her afternoon.

"It was very relaxing; I lounged in the sun and read poetry."

I asked, "What did Sadie make you for lunch?"

"I wasn't too hungry, so I just had tea."

"Well, Anna, I need to do the evenin' chores first, but I hope dinner is more than tea; I will be famished after all that hard work."

I went down to the barn and put the horses up for the night. I gave them water and hay; the cattle were still out to pasture. I made sure the chicken coop was secure. I didn't want a fox eatin' my breakfast or the hens.

It was a fine evenin' and still warm— nice weather for the end of April. Maybe Anna would like to go up to the ridge and stargaze for a bit after dinner. I headed up to the house as dinner was callin' my name.

Sadie had left my dinner on the table with a note that she had headed home and would see me in the morning. Dinner smelled delicious. Fried chicken, mashed potatoes, gravy, and homemade biscuits. She even had collard greens and bread puddin' on the table . . . *if I did not love Anna so much I might try and steal Sadie away from her husband*, I thought to myself with a chuckle.

As soon as dinner was over, I cleared the table and asked Anna, "Do you want to head up to the ridge and stargaze: it is an unusually warm evenin' and so clear."

"I love to stargaze, Seth, but I would prefer to stay in tonight. I heard there was rain tonight in the forecast."

I did not recall hearin' about rain, but ya' never know, a

storm can blow up in a heartbeat out here and flash floods are common, especially along Galisteo Creek. Motorists are always gettin' washed away along U.S. 285 when there is heavy rain. I acquiesced, and we headed into the den where I settled in beside her on the big leather sofa.

"Seth, would you read to me from one of my poetry books?"

This time she was requesting the poem, *What the Living Do* by Marie Howe. How could I deny her anything? I began:

> *"It's winter again: the sky's a deep, headstrong blue, and the sunlight pours through the open living-room windows because the heat's on too high in here and I can't turn it off. For weeks now, driving, or dropping a bag of groceries in the street, the bag breaking, I've been thinking: This is what the living do. And yesterday, hurrying along those wobbly bricks in the Cambridge sidewalk, spilling my coffee down my wrist and sleeve . . ."*

I looked down at Anna, and she seemed a million miles away, lost in her thoughts. "Anna," I said.

"Hmmm," she replied.

"Just wonderin' where you went."

"I am here; I just love the sound of your voice as you read

to me, and I also was wondering how someone can take everyday things that are so ordinary and make them sound extraordinary; Marie is gifted."

I love her fascination with poetry that is so ordinary. I feel that she is the reason it becomes extraordinary. Her adoration of the prose makes me notice how mundane, yet beautiful life can be, even when we are doing the most boring of tasks.

I told her, "I am ready for bed as daylight is goin' to be upon us sooner than we think."

She grudgingly got up, and we headed to bed.

Tonight's dream consisted of some very sensual acts. Anna was dressed scantily in her negligee, and she was silhouetted by the light of the bathroom as she stood in the doorway. She sauntered over to the bed and crawled across it to me. She stroked my belly and then sensually placed her hand around me. She clasped me and began to slowly twist her hand while strokin'. And as she continued, she began teasin' me with her tongue and the rest . . . well, is too private to share.

The mornin' intruded like a freight train, and I wished I could continue to bask in the languid dream realm forever! "The cattle are callin', and if I don't get up, they will be bawlin'! Time for work!" I said as I dragged on my clothes.

Anna was still lying in bed; I teased her that she was being lazy today. She said, "I like to sleep in on rainy days." She had been right; the rain began during the night, now softly tappin' on the metal roof and windows.

Sadie was happily cookin' away in the kitchen; she made biscuits and gravy, very filling, true comfort food. "Good Mornin' Sadie!" I looked out of the window and saw that it was rainin' harder than I thought.

"Good Morning, Boss."

"I didn't notice it being a downpour upstairs. Well, I better head into the mudroom and get my rain gear on." I walked to the barn and flipped on the radio as I fed and groomed the horses. A Chris Ledoux song, *"The Ride"* was playin'; he is one of my favorites. I sure miss him, but his son, Ned, has been doing a few of Chris's songs at rodeos and other events Out West since his father passed a few years ago. He is just as good as his dad was. One of the verses in the song is so profound to me . . .

"Sit tall in the saddle and hold your head up high, keep your eyes fixed . . . where the trail meets the sky, live like you ain't afraid to die, don't be scared. . . just enjoy your ride. I know someday farther down the road I will come to the edge of the great unknown, there stands a black horse riderless, I will wonder if I am ready for this, I will saddle him up and he will twitch his tail and I will tip my hat and bid farewell . . ."

Time for me to get on my riderless horse and face this gloomy day. I mounted Chase. "Let's go, old friend, giddy up." I rode toward the north ridge with the rain slappin' me in the face and wishin' I could have stayed in bed with Anna.

I found a cow down in the back forty acres of the ridge; she was in labor and havin' trouble. I got off of Chase, secured him, and went to see what I could do for her. I was able to reach inside of her and get the baby turned, as he had been breech, instead of his front legs and head, he was coming out with his bottom first. I did my best to be gentle, but the rain was drippin' in my eyes, it was slippery in the mud, and the calf's hooves must have punctured the mother's birth canal. She started to hemorrhage. I was too far from the house and barn to get cell service— no time to call the vet. I tried to help her, but my efforts were futile. I had to put the calf on my saddle to bring him back to the barn. I would have to feed him tonight and then tried to get a cow to adopt him. There were a few heifers that had lost their calves. That would be tomorrow's work though; today I had to get this little guy back and get him dry, warm and fed.

I filled a stall with straw, nice and deep, so he would feel safe and warm. I rigged up a heat lamp, took out a cloth, and rubbed him dry. Luckily we kept powdered milk for the orphaned calves. I got the teat bottle out, turned on the tap in the kitchenette to get some warm water, measured out the amount of powder needed for the bottle, and went back to the stall. It was such a pleasure to feed the calf and listen to him sucklin' while I held him, a poor baby, without a mother. The will to survive sure is strong. After feedin' him, I left to finish the night checks.

Next week would be the time when we had a big round up to get the herd vaccinated, wormed, and tagged and branded the new stock. For now, I had to focus on this little guy. "What can we call you, little fellow?" I decided to name him Frank after my uncle who had passed away when I was about twelve. He was a great man, a boxer, a fighter, and I knew this little guy had the spirit of a fighter. He would be okay.

I was wet, tired, cold, and could not wait to get inside where the fire was blazin' warm and there was food to fill my grumblin' belly. I knew I was in for a long night havin' to get up to feed Frank every two hours, I sure hoped tomorrow one of the cows would adopt him . . . if not, it would be a long few months to come.

Anna remarked, "You look like a drowned rat!"

"You are soooo funny." I went up to take a bath and asked her to join me.

"Sure, I would love to."

We headed upstairs, and I added some white sage bath bubbles for her. We got in, and it felt so good I dozed off; the dream was so enticin' I could have stayed there in the tub all night. Anna and I makin' gentle waves in the water as our bodies rocked back and forth in the sudsy foam . . . mmmm, pure heaven. I came to, and she was dryin' herself off with a towel.

"Come on, cowboy, time to eat; your supper is waiting on the table."

We entered the kitchen, and I told her about the calf named Frank. She insisted on comin' to the barn after supper to watch me feed him. I yawned, "Well, first, I need to make a strong pot of coffee for the night to come, as it is gonna be a long one!"

She seemed excited about the prospect; I, on the other hand, felt a wave of exhaustion. Supper was the remedy for the hard day I'd had; Sadie's vittles were the cure to many an ailment. She had made a simple pot roast, but the butter meltin' on the potatoes and vegetables with a little salt and pepper was a delight to my taste buds. She had made a homemade apple pie for dessert. The apples that we had canned last fall came from the orchard. The biscuits were so flaky and light they almost melted in my mouth. I wanted to curl up by the fire and cuddle with Anna, but Frank waited.

We entered the barn, and Frank—a lonely little boy wantin' his basic needs met—was bawlin' softly. I readied the bottle as Anna watched me settle in with the calf in my lap to feed him.

She commented, "Seth, you are so soft and gentle when you want to be."

"I guess it comes natural, I was raised by a lovin' set of parents, my mom was affectionate, and my father always made sure to tuck us in and read a story to us when he was able. He was a businessman and often had late meetins', but when he was home, he always tucked us in.

"My brother and I are only two years apart; he is my junior. I miss him as he went abroad to study and loved it so much that he stayed. He lives in the U.K. After obtainin' his degree at Oxford, he stayed on at the university workin' for them. He met and married a nice girl from Edinburgh, Scotland. She was at Oxford with him. Her name is Alpina; he is Sandoval, Sandy for short.

"We are two different entities for sure. Sandy always loved crunchin' numbers and works as the administrator of financial aid at Oxford admissions. Alpina was working there as a lecturer in Biology until she became pregnant; now, she is content to be a stay at home mom. Sandy also has done some investin' and is quite well off due to him being savvy with his investments. Their daughter, Angeline, is growin' up too fast. I wish they could visit while I am here on the ranch and meet you, Anna."

He gazed at Anna, "Maybe someday we too will have a little girl, and they could grow up together. Well maybe . . . someday."

I brought my attention back to Frank; he was hungrily suckin' on the fake teat, and once he had his fill, we headed back to bed.

I had a fitful night havin' to get up every two hours to feed Frank and was a bit grouchy the next mornin', especially not having my normal erotic dreams. Those make my nights in Galisteo memorable.

Before I met Anna, I would be alone out here, except for Sadie or the occasional hired hand comin' in when needed. I did go to Madrid for some fun now and again, but it was not the same as the life I live now. I feel complete fulfillment with hard work, good food, and a lovin' partner. I may ask Anna to marry me one day soon.

The next week was uneventful, just more of the same ole' same ole'. Anna lookin' lovely every day, work continued in the barn, and, out on the range, Sadie's great cookin', and nights full of eroticism! I was settlin' into a groove. I gave Anna a heads up, "Tomorrow is the cattle drive to bring 'em in close so we can vaccinate and brand 'em. I would like to invite some of the other wives and girlfriends to come stay with you while we are out doin' the roundup and workin' for the next few days. For us men . . . we are goin' to be sleepin' under the stars, eatin' beans and drinkin' strong coffee while workin' until we are weary to our bones."

"Awww, Seth, I really am not in the mood for company, but if it would make you happy, I can play hostess for the next few days."

"Okay, I will put a few feelers out to see if the ladies bite."

I called the guys and asked if their wives and girlfriends would like to join them, and they explained that the girls already have a standin' date to have a girl's spa weekend in Albuquerque. They assured me that Anna would certainly be welcome to join them. I thanked them and doubtfully replied, "I will run it by Anna and get back with you."

After I fed the calf and finished my chores, I went in to eat and talk to Anna about the girl's spa day. "Of course," she lamented, "It would be wonderful, but I would not be comfortable with a group of women I do not know, and I don't like to drive alone to Albuquerque."

"Well, I can have Sadie take you in; I bet she would love a spa day."

She insisted, "I would be uncomfortable, and I want to stay home and read. I can take a bubble bath here, and it will be just the same as if I am at the spa."

I did not want to force the issue and hated the thought of her in this big ranch house all alone at night, but she assured me, "I will be just fine, don't worry."

The guys arrived just before daybreak, unloaded their horses, and packed their gear on the pack mules. Jake unloaded his chuckwagon from the flatbed and his team of draft horses; he was to be our kitchen for the next three days— longer if we have any unforeseen issues arise out there. After all, there are about 2,500 heads out there, and the ranch is also surrounded by state grazin' land so there is a vast area that we will be roundin' up the herd from. Three days is probably not long enough, but I did not want to be away from Anna for too long. I plan to push the men to get it done.

Frank was adopted by a cow this mornin', and I don't need

to worry about his care now 'cuz his surrogate momma will take good care of the little guy.

Once the group got organized, we set off; the wagon will have to be stationed on a road near where we are workin' as we will be goin' up and down mountains and hills and in and out of canyons. I am grateful that the weather cleared as the added threat of a flash flood is never fun on the yearly cattle drive. The other issue is a stampede; they are rare but can happen. In fact, there is another Chris Ledoux song aptly titled *"Stampede"* about just that.

We rode to the north ridge and began gatherin' the cows and calves, roundin' them up, and takin' them to the holdin' pens. About four hundred and fifty head were in close for birthin'; the rest of the herd was scattered across the ranch and would take a bit of time to find. A few of the cowhands will stay with the cows and calves as they must be fed now that they are in holdin' pens, and they can also start the vaccinations and taggin' that needs to be done. They will have to log all the work, so we know who has been done and who has not.

Ridin' the range is a great time to practice a little introspection. Before landin' here at the Ames Ranch, I thought my life was goin' nowhere. A literal dead-end street. I worked as a horseback ridin' guide and lived in a teepee on the property where the stable was located; at least, I had a place to sleep, food in my belly, and a jingle in my pocket.

Meetin' Anna gave me purpose; it has changed the course of my life, and now I feel I am headed in the right direction. I can see a future, and that is the best feelin' a man can have. I make an honest livin', have a good woman, and I am starin' at a bright future. I normally don't say too many blessings, but lately, I am grateful to the Lord above for all of the Love that has been shown me. I heard a yell comin' from the left of me, so I looked over, and I saw Hank wavin' at me and hollerin' to get my attention. I galloped over to see what the ruckus was about.

"Hank, what is all the noise about?" I inquired.

"Seth, I just saw someone take off down there at the bottom of the ridge. He isn't part of this outfit, and I thought I better alert you. Have you been havin' trouble with rustlers lately?"

"I haven't noticed anything out of the ordinary." Lately, I've been so wrapped up in Anna that I wasn't lookin' either. I told Hank, "We better holler at the others to be on the lookout for anything suspicious, and I will ride down to the bottom and take a look around." I wish I had a way to get word to Anna that she should go into town for a few days with Sadie just to be safe.

I rode down the ridge and saw a few hoof prints in the sand and a cigarette butt, but nothin' really alarmin'. It could have just been a teenager out for a ride and a smoke, far away from their parents. I would be more alert while we were out here though just in case. *What could anyone want off this ranch*? I thought to myself.

I pondered that for a moment . . . *well, maybe the cattle. Since the owner is away and the bank took over the note, people feel a little bit less poorly about stealin' from the bank than they do a neighbor.*

After we got the cattle rounded up and settled down, we laid out the bedrolls and lit the campfire. It felt good to have some grub and coffee, and then lay down under the stars. There was nothin' like the huge blanket of twinklin' lights out here away from the city's light pollution, you can almost see clear to heaven. Tommy got out his guitar and played a few songs, nice quiet music for bedtime.

I thought that all people should experience this at least once in their lifetime. I began to think about Anna and if she had ever camped out here as a child . . .

I dozed off with her on my mind, and then I had another dream: Anna was lyin' on the bedroll with me under the stars. The campfire was cracklin', and the wind was makin' a swishin' sound through the trees. A cow would bawl soft and low now and then . . .

Anna was astride me. As she leaned in to kiss me, her soft blonde hair brushed my face, and the scent of jasmine filled my senses. I felt her butterfly light kisses across my lips, and then she moved down to my neck and started to unbutton my shirt leavin' a trail of soft kisses all the way down until I felt her breath lower, and I could not take it anymore. Overtakin' her, I grabbed her and rolled us, so she was on the bottom now; she moaned with every thrust, and I thought I could be lost in her forever.

The hot sun on my face awoke me bright and early, my dream had been so vivid and real that I expected to see Anna beside me; I was sadly disappointed when I realized it was just Hank.

We packed up the bedrolls and headed over to see what Jake had made for breakfast. We all complained a bit when it was a grey gruel that he swore was oatmeal. We ate it anyway and drank some strong coffee, and then it was back in the saddle again.

The sun was hot, and it felt like my thirst would never be quenched. I drank enough water to drown an elephant today. I was happy to see the last cow straggle in and be accounted for; now, we could push them back to the holdin' area and get them all vaccinated, wormed, tagged, and branded. *It may take a day more than,* he thought, *but at least they would be back closer to the barn and bunkhouse for that part of the work.*

We got all of the cattle into the holdin' pens and began the task of brandin' after all of them had been vaccinated, wormed, and tagged. It was one of those tedious jobs that start to become automated, but as soon as you got in a groove, a rank cow would kick you back into gear! I felt as battered and bruised as the rest of the crew looked by the time the sun set. We still had about a hundred head to finish in the mornin'.

Another night out in the open: we went about the routine of layin' out the bedrolls, eatin', and sippin' some strong coffee around the campfire while Tommy played his guitar. I thought to myself that at least my nights were very pleasant. I smelled smoke in the air. I noted that none of my crew smoked cigarettes. Fred smoked a pipe, but that was definitely smoke from a cigarette I smelled. I made the motion for the guys to be quiet and carry on as I snuck away into the shadows. I saw a young man smokin' down a way from camp. He had his horse tied to a tree and was leanin' against that same tree.

I snuck up on the boy, "Hey, what are you doing lurkin' around this ranch?"

"My name is Brandon, but folks call me Ma'ii, it is Navajo for Coyote," the boy explained. "My mom used to play here as a child and has told me several stories about it. She said she used to bring me here when I was a baby, but I don't remember it. I wanted to experience it also, as her stories intrigued me."

"I see," I replied.

"I come here often, but normally there is no one around to see me. I was scared the other day and thought you guys might have been a gang rustling the cattle since the place was all but abandoned. That is why I lit outta here."

"Well, glad to make your acquaintance, Ma'ii. I am Seth, the caretaker." I continued to lecture him on the perils of smokin'.

The response I got was, "I know, I know . . . my mom hates it; that's why I smoke here!"

I introduced him to the gang after I took him back to the campfire and continued to ask him about himself. Ma'ii was a gifted guitar player; he went to his horse and slipped his guitar from the side of his saddle where he had attached it with a custom carrier he had made especially for it, and joined Tommy for a few songs.

Later Ma'ii wanted to teach Tommy a song from the Tanoan language, which had been spoken here many years ago. It is a mixture of the Aztec and other tribes that joined together in this area.

"There are many abandoned ruins from the people of that time; the language family has seven languages from four branches, Tewa, Jemez, Kiowa, and Tiwa," he added. "The words were about the limitless natural resources and how the people used them in their 'mystery' pouches which hung around their necks for protection. These were considered 'good medicine' and often had a stone or rock in them; the item could also be a piece of bone, a button, or any object that was precious to the wearer. They normally were fastened around the neck when stealing horses for a successful theft, and ironically the owner of the horses wore one to block the theft as well."

He strummed his guitar for effect. "The song I will sing is truly about good and bad being two sides of one coin. As the Tonoan peoples believed that everything had good and bad within it, even animals and locales. They also believed that Nature's moods coincided with this good and bad theme," he continued. "If you visited some of the abandoned sites, you could see evidence of the many mysteries spoken about in the songs shown in the pictographs, many containing strange people, such as dwarfs, giants, and witches.

"There are also many other symbols as well; there are very few birds in other ruins, but birds are depicted here in the basin, and no one knows why other sites have few. There are some that represent the Phoenix or the Eagle at sites in Sedona, Arizona, because of tribal names, but other birds are non-existent in sites in that area, although there are many other animals, especially turtles and deer at those sites."

Ma'ii wished to be an archeologist or anthropologist when he grew up, he said. He told the men, "The ancient ways mesmerize me, and I love learning about them. I also love to go to the abandoned sites and soak up the energy held there; it is alive with the 'mysteries' of the people that lived there many moons before us."

I asked, "Would you like to join us, or would your mother be worried about you?"

He replied, "She has no idea I am not at home. I often wait until she falls asleep, then I sneak out to the barn and saddle up my horse, hiding behind him until I am in the clear to mount up and ride out to the 'mystery' places. I have only been hangin' around here because I saw the activity and fires; I was just keepin' an eye out."

I told him, "I will call your mother in the mornin' when we wake up."

Brandon replied, "That would be fine as she works at the Lamay railroad station as a guide for the tourists who come here to see the ruins. She is up early every day because she has to be ready for her first tours by eight in the morning."

The next day upon wakin', I placed the call, assuring Brandon's mother, Catori, that the boy was in good hands and we could use him for the last bit of work. Also, I would feed him and give him a little compensation for his work. I then asked her about her name, "What does Catori mean?"

She told me, "It is Hopi, meaning spirit; most people just call me Tori though. I will swing by after work to meet you and check on Brandon."

"I look forward to it." After disconnectin', I thought this would be a wonderful chance for Anna to meet someone who could be a friend. I felt she was too isolated out here on this big ol' ranch.

After the last cow was branded, we turned the herd loose and headed back to the barn.

I told Ma'ii, "You can put your horse up in a stall. I only have the two horses in the equine barn; there are quite a few open stalls to choose from. That way you can wash up and be ready when your mom comes to check on you."

I invited all of the men to come on in and enjoy some of

Sadie's good cookin,' but they were all ready to head home. They missed their families. The guys packed up and headed out.

Brandon loved Sadie's vittles, as he called them. He said, "I would be willing to help out here and be paid in her cooking."

"I agree that she is gifted, and you could do just that; this is a big spread for one man to handle." I felt that the boy needed a male role model in his life as he seemed to be on his own most of the time. Raisin' a child alone was hard nowadays—especially when the single parent had to work and a mother raisin' a boy was even tougher.

Catori came by around eight in the evening. She explained, "Often my tours run over as people like to ask questions, and hangin' out with them socially brings in more tips, which are needed in today's economy."

When she came in the kitchen, she kissed Brandon on his forehead, to which he whined, "Mom, you are treating me like a child."

She retorted, "Well, you are MY child!"

"Mom, I am a man now!" She could not get used to the fact that her little boy WAS growing up!

I could not help but notice Tori's dark, good looks. Where

Anna was light, blonde with eyes the color of the sky, Tori was dark, her hair almost black, and her eyes a green-grey mixture.

Brandon got his mother's good looks and eye color, but his skin and hair are much lighter than hers. They both were slim and tall. Like mother, like son. I thought that Anna and I would have a towhead if they ever had a baby, even though I am dark-haired and green-eyed. I had been blonde when he was young. His hair has darkened with age.

I asked Tori, "Have you eaten?"

"No, I actually am hungry."

I brought her a plate from the leftovers. I had wanted to introduce her to Anna, but she was in bed with a headache. She told me to let them know she was sorry that she could not come down to meet them, but her migraine made it impossible for her to be out of her darkened room.

While Tori ate her supper, I asked her about her life. I said, "Ma'ii has told me that you are a tour guide for the Santa Fe Railroad service, which brings tourists down to the ruins."

She affirmed, "Yes, I have a degree in anthropology, and I love being outside, so this was a better choice of employment than working in a stuffy museum or an office."

I also asked her about the time she spent on this ranch and hoped she could enlighten me a bit about the events that led the ranch to be in its current state.

Tori said, "Yes, I had spent most of my time here as a child. Originally I lived in Farmington on the Navajo reservation, one of the largest reservations in the four corners area. It is the place where Arizona, Utah, New Mexico, and Colorado meet. Yet the people call it 'Totah,' the place where three rivers meet. The area was founded by ancestral peoples, consisting of Ute, Anasazi, Jicarilla Apaches, and Navajo. . ."

I laughed, "Do you always give a history lesson when explainin' where you are from?"

She blushed, "I like to include my heritage as it is important to me. I am proud of my people."

I explained, "I was just teasin' you, no need to get so worked up about it."

Ma'ii had went to the barn to check on his horse and gather his belongings. He would leave his horse there as part of the deal he had made with me. The adults headed out to the barn together to get him so that Tori could get home. Her days are long, and she had to be up early tomorrow as she does every day, six days a week.

I apologized, "I regret that you didn't get to meet Anna; I had hoped you would become fast friends, but maybe next time, as Anna has a headache and is restin'."

Tori looked at him quizzically, "The name Anna always stirs emotion in me being that was my childhood friend's name, the one whom I played with on this ranch, but sadly she has passed."

I said, "Well, that is an odd coincidence."

We arrived at the barn and helped Brandon load up his things. He had put his saddle in the tack room and fed and watered the horses for me. I thanked him and watched as they drove off in his mom's Jeep Renegade. I thought, *What a cute little car! It suited her.*

Tori was stunned by Seth's good looks, tall, rugged, and handsome. He was, with dark hair, green eyes, and just a bit of that five o'clock shadow, he was strong and lean. *He must be about six three,* she thought, *every girl's dream. Anna was a lucky woman.*

Having the evenin' chores done gave me some time to be with Anna. We had not had quality time in almost a week! I headed up to my room.

Anna was sleepin'. I thought about wakin' her but instead decided to do some snoopin' around the house. First order of business was to find the key to the only locked room in the house. I searched through all of the keys hangin' on the hooks in the mudroom and could not locate one that fit the lock on that room. I decided that it most likely would be in the study, probably in the desk that Silas used when he ran this spread.

I sat down at the desk; it was rich mahogany and handcrafted, very impressive, and truly a work of art. I pondered where to start. I decided upon the top drawer center, I pulled it out and searched through the contents, just normal desk items, pens, pencils, a few paper clips, business cards, etc. nothing that even resembled a key. I ran my hands along the top, bottom, sides, and edges to no avail.

If I were going to hide a key, where would I put it? I thought if it was I, I would put it in the middle drawer, as usually people do the top or bottom, but never the middle. I opened the middle drawer.

I found files, most were on the ranch hands, their background checks, pay, etc. One was of interest to me; it contained some information on the daughter. I decided to read it later, right now I wanted to see what was in that room.

I ran my hand along the top of the drawer, the bottom of the drawer, and I felt a bump. I felt around and it was a key shape that had been taped up with a strong adhesive, probably duct tape. I found the edge and peeled the tape back feelin' the key drop into my hand.

I took it upstairs and was just about to open the door when Anna appeared in the hallway. She asked, "Seth, can you come to bed now? I really have missed you, and it is a comfort to have you near when I am feeling poorly." He pocketed the key and headed toward her.

"Sure darlin', anything to make my girl happy." The mystery of the locked door would have to wait.

I stripped off my clothes and slid in next to Anna. I wrapped myself around her like a cocoon; she felt warm and soft, just like a woman should.

She snuggled against me, and I drifted off to sleep; it had been a rough week, and this was heaven compared to the open ground. I loved my Galisteo nights a lot more than my Galisteo days. Anna, soft and supple, willin' to please me in any way I wished, always came to me in my dreams. Her blonde hair tumblin' in my face smellin' of night jasmine as she softly brushed against my penis. I could not hold back and penetrated her, becoming' one with her. Too soon I was openin' my eyes and facing the day. Anna felt better today and joined me for breakfast.

She listened intently as I described the roundup in detail; she became reticent when I got to the part about Brandon and Tori though.

I questioned, "Anna, you seem upset, what is it, my love?"

She said nothing, but he persisted. She said, "I don't like you spending time with another woman or caring for her child."

I thought this was a side of Anna I had not seen, and I was sure I did not like it at all. "Anna, there is no need to be jealous; you know I love you, and the boy needs some male influence in his life.

He is alone too much. I also can use the help around here."

She conceded and changed the subject. She wanted to know how the horses were. She asked, "Can we take a ride this evening?"

"I would love to; it would be nice to ride up on the ridge and stargaze after the week of work I've had." I had somethin' to look forward to now; I happily whistled as I set off for the barn.

Ma'ii was just a bit late as his mom had to drop him off at the road and it was a hike back to the barn. "She needed to get to work," he said.

I said, "Ya' know, I think there is an old four-wheeler out in the equipment shed. I prefer to ride the fences on horseback and don't use it. After our chores let's go see if it runs and if so, tune it up for you. If it is ok with your mom, you can use it to get to and from work, which will take the burden off of her so she can focus on getting' to her own job."

The boy's eyes lit up like the northern lights. I was glad he suggested it.

With two people, it took half the time to get the chores tended to.

Ma'ii asked, "Might I have a break to go up and eat some of Sadie's delectables? My mom did not have time to feed me breakfast."

"Delectables?" I raised my eyebrow at Brandon.

Brandon replied, "Yes, it is my word of the day. I try to learn a new word each day, and today it is delectable."

We both laughed as we headed to the house. After I got Brandon situated in the kitchen, I left him in the capable hands of Sadie while I went to look for Anna. If she met the boy, she couldn't help but love him.

I found her on the opposite side of the house in the garden; she loved the flowers and herbs planted there and spent a lot of time here. I asked her, "Come in and meet Brandon, please?"

She agreed. We went into the house and when we got to the kitchen, we encountered only Sadie. I asked after the boy.

"He was so excited about getting the four-wheeler that he headed out to the barn to get you. He told me he could not wait for you guys to get to work on it."

"Well, I better head down there; heaven knows I don't want to leave him alone to do the job!" I brushed Anna's cheek with a kiss and headed out, "Anna, if you want, come on down to the barn and I can introduce you."

"Maybe in a bit, I want to spend a bit more time in the garden."

Sadie thought to herself, *what on earth goes on in that man's head?* She liked her job, so decided to keep her opinions to herself, but for the life of her, he did some odd things. She would continue to mind her own business, yet she hoped he would meet a nice girl and perhaps stay on here, which would give her job security, maybe the boy's mother? She went back to cleaning up the kitchen and preparing lunch.

Brandon and I had cleaned the four-wheeler and put gas in it, checked the oil, and after a few unsuccessful attempts it sputtered and roared to life! I insisted on giving the boy a lesson in safety and instruction for driving.

Ma'ii said, "I know how to drive!"

I insisted, and after the lesson, they parked the vehicle and headed to the barn where Brandon cleaned stalls, and I made repairs to the tack.

CHAPTER TWO

Later we saddled up the horses and headed out to check fences. On the way up to the ridge I asked Brandon, "Why do you prefer to be called Ma'ii?"

"Because I am like the coyote, a loner, and very observant."

"If that is what you like to be called, then I will try to use it more often," He added. "Why does your mom call you Brandon if you prefer Ma'ii?"

"Because she insists on calling me by the name she has given me at birth," was all he said.

I found my thoughts going to Tori. I found her attractive and exotic with her dark looks, the opposite of Anna with all of her lightness. I was even looking forward to seeing her again. I asked Ma'ii, "Do you think you and your mom would like to come over on

Sunday for a barbeque? It is Sadie's day off that day, so we like to BBQ."

Ma'ii looked anxious to come. "I am partial to Sadie's cooking, but a BBQ would be nice. I will check with mom."

I found myself feeling a bit guilty about my thoughts later on when Anna and I were heading up to the ridge. It was the first time anyone had entered my thoughts that way since I had met her. I reasoned with myself, *Well, I am a healthy male; I guess it is normal to fantasize about a beautiful woman, even though he was quite satisfied with his own woman.* We reached her favorite spot on the ridge, the one where they had met, dismounted, and secured the ponies, as she liked to call them.

I laid out the blanket and motioned Anna to my side. This truly was my happy place, under the stars with Anna at my side. I loved it here and was trying to find a way to buy the ranch. I wanted to live here with Anna and raise a family. I asked Anna, "How many kids do you want?"

She said, "I am not sure; I never really thought about it and I prefer to talk about something else, like the vastness of the cosmos."

I kept pursuing the subject; she turned away and began to sob softly.

I asked, "What is going on?"

She said, "I . . . I cannot have children!"

"Oh, I am sorry to push this on you and upset you, baby. I had no idea."

"Well, how could you have known?" she assured him it was alright. "I do not want to lose you, and I am hoping you understand."

"Yes, of course, our love is what matters; you are my family, Anna."

That seemed to pacify her, and we lay there in silence taking in the wonder that blanketed us above. Sometimes I felt that Anna wished she was among the stars, far away from here. Just then a star shot across the sky in a blaze, fading as it fell.

The next morning, we awoke still cuddled on the blanket on the ridge. *Odd*, I thought that I had been able to sleep soundly out here; it must have been her by my side that pacified me. It was time to get back to the house and eat before Brandon arrived. Anna and I headed back to the barn.

Anna asked, "I could you tend to my horse? I want to clean up before breakfast." She headed to the house.

A few minutes later, Ma'ii came in. I asked, "Did you pass Anna in the drive?"

The boy said, "No." He looked back at where he had come from to emphasize that there was no one there.

I thought that was odd as they must have had to walk right by one another, but as soon as I thought it, it slipped away as there were so many other thoughts that needed thinking.

I looked at Ma'ii, "Let's head up and eat before morning chores; the horses need to finish eating before they are tacked up."

When we got to the house, Anna was nowhere to be seen. I got breakfast for Ma'ii and went up to find Anna; she was in the bathroom taking a bath and told me she would be down shortly. I was starved, so I went back down to eat and wait on her. Women!

Brandon had inhaled his food and was heaping seconds on his plate! I wished I had the advantage of youth and could eat like that again, but age has a way of ruining all the fun. They ate, and Ma'ii took his dishes to the sink. "Thank you, Sadie," he said, "I will go brush the horses and get them ready for work, Seth."

Just as the door shut, Anna appeared smelling like her beloved garden. She was glowing.

I said, "Sorry, but I need to get to work baby."

"That's okay, I don't mind eating alone."

The week flew by, and soon it was Sunday. I had told Anna about the barbeque. She seemed less than excited. I was growing weary of her avoidance of company. Maybe she needed to see a therapist. She never wanted to leave the ranch and was very antisocial. She did not even talk to Sadie. As much as I loved having her to myself, I thought it odd that she only wanted to be with me. *Well, at least today she would be around some company, and I would observe her, hoping she would act normal.*

Tori and Brandon arrived just after two in the afternoon.

They brought some cornbread and a pasta salad to add to the meal. Anna came down in a sundress looking radiant.

Tori said, "Hello," and commented, "you look familiar."

Anna said, "I don't think we have met . . ."

"It may come to me; I never forget a face."

Brandon said, "Hello," to Anna also. "It is a pleasure to meet you."

Much to my surprise, the day went splendidly. Anna and Tori hit it off just as I had hoped; they laughed and talked like two teenage girls. It was great to see her so happy, and it eased my mind to see Anna finally interact with other people.

For Anna the afternoon was a delight, she felt happy to have a female friend, and she was certain she had met Tori previously but felt it best to act as if she hadn't. The time would surely come when Tori would recall their meeting, but until then she decided to just get reacquainted.

We all decided to have a bonfire and make s'mores in the evening. Of course, Brandon had four! A growing boy. Tori had one, and she looked cute with marshmallow dripping down her chin! They all laughed about that. Anna never ate sweets, but I fantasized about her having marshmallow dripping from her sweet pink lips.

Finally, it was time for Tori to go, so we said their goodbyes and she and Brandon left.

I was so pleased with the day's events that I picked Anna up and twirled her around; we headed to bed laughing as we climbed the stairs two at a time. We fell on the bed in a passionate embrace and we drifted off to sleep just like that . . .

I, of course, had one of my wonderful night visits from Anna. Aaaah, the sweet pleasures she imparted, just as I fantasized earlier. She had a bit of marshmallow dripping from her lip; she took some melted chocolate and put it on his penis, slowly licking it off of me. I was so hard that I felt the need to get released.

I toppled Anna onto the bed and shoved into her as if I was impaling her. Anna gasped but matched my rhythm thrust for thrust until we both lay spent.

Somewhere during the night, the dream changed, and I saw Tori standing in the background watching them. These dreams just got better and better!

Another week went by, and it seemed that the boy and I were growing closer and closer. On the weekends, Brandon and his mom often stopped in to visit, and on Saturday, Anna asked them to stay over and have brunch the next morning.

I was shocked and pleased as they agreed. They had another fire, this time without the s'mores. She and Ma'ii told stories about the ruins and the mysteries of the tribes. There was intrigue in the air. Anna loved mysteries. Brandon even played his guitar for them while crooning softly in Navajo. It was so enjoyable.

We all decided to do a bit of stargazing, so we laid out a

blanket and looked up at the stars. We saw several shooting stars and made wishes. Sadly, it was getting late and our eyes were growing weary. Anna showed them to their guest rooms and everyone turned in for the night.

Tonight, my dream took an unexpected turn; my Galisteo nights just became hotter. I was lying on the bed. He was throbbing as Tori and Anna danced around the room naked, bathed in the moonlight. Anna slowly crawled across the bed to lay kisses down my chest and stomach; she beckoned Tori to join us. Tori lay down beside me as Anna reached over me and kissed her softly on her lips and then began to suckle her breast. It was almost too much for me; I slipped my fingers inside of Tori as Anna remained stimulating her breasts . . . Tori and Anna switched places, soon they were taking turns straddling me and kissing me, while I was pleasuring the one on my side by immersing my fingers within her softness until she shuddered and moaned. Then the girls would change places . . . I awoke in a sweat and felt exhausted.

As we went down to prepare brunch, I was glad it was Sunday as I was spent; there would be no energy to work today. I asked Ma'ii, "Can you tend to the horses while the adults prepare the food?"

To my surprise, Anna chipped in; she always told me she abhorred cooking and cleaning! I was certainly enjoying these new changes. We all sat down to eat as soon as Ma'ii rejoined the group.

I asked Tori if she knew anything about the history of the ranch. She told him, "I was born in Farmington and my mother met a man who worked in the silver mines in Cerrillos. He married her, and she and I moved to this area when she was about eight. My stepfather lost his job due to developing an illness that made it impossible for him to go down into the mines. His long exposure to silver dust and other silver compounds had created breathing problems along with an enlarged heart.

"That was when Silas hired him on here at the ranch as a foreman for the hands. He had an office in the barn and was able to handle the ranch business and oversee the men. I spent many hours here because my mother worked as a housekeeper for another ranch in the area. My stepfather, Barry, would bring me to work so I could play with the owner's daughter, whose name was also Anna, and we became best friends."

Anna asked, "What became of your friend?"

Tori replied, "She has passed on, there was a horrible accident, a flash flood at the Galisteo Creek on U. S. 285. It had been raining heavily and Anna was driving; the rain was so strong that she must not have been able to see the water on the road. It was nighttime, her car was swept up and it flipped over, landing in the creek . . . she drowned."

I could see it was upsetting Tori to talk about it, and he looked at Anna about to change the subject, and she also looked pale and grief-stricken. "I suggest we discuss a lighter topic."

Everyone agreed and began to talk about the weather: it was heading into fall, and the temps were hot now but substantially cooler in the evenings, giving a blessed reprieve from the daytime sun.

Ma'ii said, "I would like to take my horse out and visit the ruins."

I chimed in, "I would like to learn more about the Tonoan mysteries and will join you thus giving the girls a chance to do 'girly' things." The boys headed out to the barn and soon were on their way.

Anna asked Tori, "What do you do for a living? Tori explained her job, and Anna then asked, "What is it like to raise a child alone?"

Tori told her, "It is a blessing and a curse. I love my son and yet, it is very difficult to give him the time he needs or to fill in for the male influence a father could give him."

Tori asked, "Do you and I plan on having children?"

Anna became quiet and sadness overtook her, "I am not able to conceive."

Tori sympathized with Anna. Anna then asked about Brandon's father.

Tori looked sad now, "It was not a good situation. I had him at a young age; I gave birth at fifteen.

Anna persisted, "Why would his father have abandoned

him?"

Tori began to cry saying through her tears, "My stepfather abused me, and my child was conceived because of his raping me. It is a horrible memory, but I could not get 'rid' of my baby boy. No matter how he came to be, I vowed to raise him and love him." She confided in Anna, "That is why I was always here at the ranch; it was more so he, my stepfather, had easy access to me away from my mother than it was to provide me with a playmate."

Anna searched her memory and she remembered something from her childhood. She told Tori, "I also played on this ranch as a child, I remember you now!"

Tori exclaimed, "I knew I knew you, too!"

"I heard you crying once in the tack room and had gone in to ask you what was wrong," she said. "Tori, you told me your stepfather was punishing you. Had I known what was actually going on, I would have reported it to my father. Tori, I am so sorry." She continued. "But I remember you by a different name."

"Yes, my birth name is Catori, and my stepfather liked it because it was unusual. He insisted on calling me by my full name, while everyone else called me Tori."

"But I called you Catori also . . ."

Tori recalled, "There was another girl named Anna here and that is what she called me. . . that was how I had been introduced to people by my father." Such an odd sensation swept over Tori, but she shook it off.

We guys were enjoying ourselves out at the ruins. Ma'ii had brought me to the San Cristobal Puebla ruins; they were the best known of the Galisteo Basin's pueblo ruins.

Ma'ii explained, "The San Cristobal Pueblo contained eight to nine-room 'blocks' several stories in height, organized around five ceremonial plazas. Like all other pueblos, San Cristobal had a ceremonial kiva—a large round (partly underground) structure—in its largest plaza. Two kivas north of Galisteo Creek may have been used by winter and summer groups. It is estimated that by 1400 A.D., the San Cristobal Pueblo was home to 500-1,000 people."

I was amazed at the knowledge held within the young man's head! I asked Ma'ii, "What is your age?

"Fourteen, well, I am thirteen, but my birthday is coming up in September, on the eleventh."

I wondered how old his mother was . . . *she must be around Anna's age; he wondered if they had played together on the ranch as they must have been here at about the same time.* I decided we should head back as it was getting late and everyone had work tomorrow. *Well, except his princess, Anna,* he thought as he giggled to himself. *I do spoil her.*

Everyone bid their goodnights and another wonderful day was done. I inquired, "Did you enjoy your day with Tori?"

"I did." She also told me about remembering her when they were children but did not divulge Tori's secret about her son's father.

I asked Anna, "Perhaps you would like to go into Madrid next Friday, as there is a band I like comin' to town."

"I am not much for going to the saloon."

I decided that she had been pretty social as of late and did not press the issue. We retired for the night.

As usual, I enjoyed his dream time; I awoke refreshed the next morning. Sadie was in the kitchen whippin' up her biscuits and gravy. I couldn't wait to get the barn chores over with so I could enjoy them; they were sticking to my ribs—comfort food!

Ma'ii was already feeding the horses; he said, "Maybe I will ride George today because my horse, Cheveyo, is a bit lame." I took a look and it looked like he had a stone bruise; in a couple of days, he would be good as new if it did not turn into an abscess.

I asked, "What does Cheveyo mean?"

Ma'ii told him, "It means spirit warrior."

I remembered Tori saying her name meant spirit also, and I commented on that fact.

Ma'ii said, "Yes, hers is the female version of spirit, but my horse is named spirit warrior and it is male."

"Thank you for the language lesson; I am learning something new every day from you." I was learning as much from this boy as he was teaching him.

I told Brandon, "Finish up as there is a real treat waiting for you in the kitchen!"

Brandon could smell the food as he walked through the mudroom; it made his mouth water. He loved getting paid in Sadie's cooking! He wished his mom had time to cook and be at home more; he knew she did her best to provide for him, so he never told her about his feelings, but it would be nice if one day she could be around more. He enjoyed spending time with Anna and me but especially loved it when they all three did things together with his mom. It made him feel like he had a big family.

I brought him back from his thoughts with a question: "Do you like the biscuits and gravy?"

"Sure do! They are probably my favorite so far."

Friday rolled around and I really had my heart set on seeing my buddy's band at the Mine Shaft; it was the Dirt Band, and I loved their Rockabilly sound.

I asked Anna again, "Please come along with me to the Mineshaft."

"No," she declined.

"Would you mind if I go ahead and see them alone?"

She smiled and said, "Not at all, go and have fun."

This was the Anna I knew and loved, although she did make a snarky comment about my shaving and wearing cologne.

I drove the few miles south on Highway 14, waving as he passed my friend on horseback. He was named Matt Dillon Smith, everyone called him Dillon though. His parents had a thing for *Gun Smoke* and named him after one of the characters. *What else could he be but a cowboy?* Thought I.

I would meet up with Dillon in about an hour when he arrived at the saloon where he would tie his horse to the hitchin' post and have a great night, then ride back to Cerrillos. *Good thing that old horse, Pearl, knew her way home!*

Dillon had taken over the trail guide position vacated by me and moved into the teepee; they became friends when I trained him for the job. I hoped Dillon had remembered to bring a flashlight with him.

One time I had been riding into Madrid with Dillon to celebrate after we rescued our buddy, Hardy's, escaped tortoise, Frankie. Apparently, Frankie was a repeat offender and had broken out a few times before. This time he had scooted the lounge chair over to the new higher wall and climbed over. Dillon spotted him on a trail ride and roped him, tied him to a tree, and then called Hardy when he got back to the stables. Hardy came on his motorbike complete with sidecar; it was a model like Che' Guevara's and Hardy looked the part with a leather helmet, goggles, and a scarf flying in the wind! *What a sight we were as we were riding out to the spot where the tortoise was tied. Two cowboys on horses accompanied by a man on a motorcycle . . .*

It took two hours to reach the place where Frankie was being held captive. Hardy wrapped him in a blanket, and we helped get him into the sidecar; he must weigh over a hundred pounds. When we finished, off they went, blazing through the desert like a hallucination! Hardy gave us a reward of a hundred bucks, and we decided to go into town and live it up. We realized we had no flashlights to see on our way home! We were thankful there was a full moon.

The following day, much to our chagrin, a reporter from the Santa Fe New Mexican came and woke us up early in the morning to give an interview about Frankie's rescue. *Aaah, what a memory.*

I pulled into a parking space about a quarter mile south of the mine shaft. It was always packed with tourists. I did not mind walking a bit so I could be friendly to the passerby, waving and saying hello as he went. Tonight was extra busy as there was a fundraiser going on across the street at the Holler; a young man had crashed his motorcycle and needed long-term care that his insurance would not cover. The owner of the Holler decided to hold a fundraiser for the man's mother and donate all proceeds from his pale ale sales that night. I loved their fried green tomatoes but decided to just eat a burger at the Mine Shaft while I listened to the Dirt, as we call them around here.

As I walked onto the patio, I saw Tori sitting alone at a table, "What a pleasant surprise. May I join you?"

Of course, she wanted to know if Anna was with me asking, "Will Anna be joining us?"

I said, "Sadly no, this is not her thing."

Tori looked amazing. She had on tight blue jeans with a lacy top, a lot of turquoise jewelry, and a big turquoise belt buckle. Her boots were beautiful with a gypsy rose pattern in the leather. I asked if she had eaten, and she said she had gone to the fundraiser first for a beer and the fried green tomatoes they are famous for.

"Those are my favorite also, but it was too crowded, so I am gonna' have a burger here instead. I would starve before my order came being it was so packed over there!"

Dillon came to join us just in time as the Dirt Band was about to begin, and chit-chat was hard during their sets. We enjoyed the music and even had a dance or two before the night ended. I asked her, "Do you need a ride home?"

She said, "No, I live on Waldo Mesa Road. Only about a half-mile away. I actually like walking."

"I would be much obliged if you would allow me to see you home, as it is dark out now."

I turned and said, "Goodnight" to Dillon as he was mounting

up for his ride home. He was a bit tipsy but made it into the saddle on his second try. "Don't worry Seth, I have my flashlight!" He rode off in the moonlight. I just shook my head; some things never change.

I drove Tori to her home and waited until she was safely inside, even though this was the type of town that you never needed to lock your doors in. She was looking too tempting tonight, and I wanted to make sure she was safe; maybe it was a bit of selfish reasoning as well.

I turned around and headed back to Highway 14. It was a pleasant night with a cool breeze, and I rolled the windows down for the trip back to the ranch.

Anna was asleep when I arrived. I kissed her on the cheek, and she stirred as I got into bed, but did not awaken.

That night my dream was a completely different kind of scenario, in it. I was with Tori and Brandon, and we were riding up on the north ridge, we had a picnic and were laughing. We seemed like a family.

I was troubled when I awoke in the morning. *What was happening to me, I was not the type of man to cheat on my girl, but dreams don't lie . . . here I was coveting another woman, not just a woman, but a family with that woman, and I took them to our place; to the place where I had met Anna.* It felt as if I betrayed her, and she sensed something was wrong with me.

She asked about it, "Seth, what is wrong with you today? You seem a bit off."

I replied, "I have a bit of a hangover from my fun last night."

She chastised me for drinking too much, "That is what you get for indulging!" Then let it go, thankfully.

I had forgotten to hang the truck key in the mudroom the night before as I was a bit tipsy. I reached in my pocket to get the truck key before I went to the barn and felt the key to the locked room. I wanted to check that place out.

Anna said, "I am going to the garden."

I told her, "Okay, I have a few things to do in the house and will head down to the barn after lunch."

Brandon was tending to the horses, and he asked if he could take the four-wheeler out to check fences today.

I told him he could try it out, kinda a trial run and if it went well, I may let him do it more often.

I headed upstairs and fit the key in the lock. It worked. I slowly turned the knob and inched open the door. I found myself standing in a girls' room; it was definitely feminine.

I went over to the credenza and looked at the photographs on top of it. The young girl was blonde and blue-eyed, and she had a familiarity about her. I looked closer and saw that she closely resembled Anna . . . *perhaps Anna had a twin?* I thought.

There were photos of the blonde girl, which must be Silas's

daughter, the other Anna, and a couple with a dark-haired girl with bronze skin, who had to be Tori. It must have been taken when they were young.

I looked through a few drawers and popped my head into the adjacent bathroom, but there was nothing out of the ordinary. This room looks as if it was left untouched after Silas's daughter passed. The poor man must have been unable to let go, consumed with grief . . . he lost everything.

I heard a noise behind me and turned to see Anna in the doorway. She looked sad; she asked me, "What are you doing?"

I told her, "I heard a noise in here and found the key and came in to investigate. I thought perhaps an animal had gotten trapped inside."

She looked skeptical but seemed to buy my explanation.

I concluded, "Well, we can just lock this back up and head to lunch; all is good in here."

We went downstairs. Sadie had a beautiful taco bar spread out on the counter, and Brandon was woofing down tacos like they were M & M's! I made a plate.

Anna said, "The lettuce and the cilantro are from the garden."

To make her happy, I added those to my tacos. After I inhaled my food, I told Sadie, "These were amazing, but the pulled pork tasted a bit different than normal."

She said, "That is because it is not pulled pork; I used jackfruit instead, and it is healthier for you."

It actually was good, and I did feel the need to eat lighter as my belt needed to be let out a notch recently.

Anna said she had eaten before coming up to get me.

I replied, "Okay," and turned my attention to Ma'ii. "How was the excursion on the four-wheeler this morning?"

"Excellent!"

"After lunch, we can ride out together and check it out."

He whined a bit about doubling the work but conceded as I said I would not let him do it again if I wasn't satisfied with the results. He told me, "I found a fox sneaking around by the barn earlier and chased it away." He added, "The fence is holdin' strong and I found no areas that need repair."

I said, "Okay, we will see, and if all is as you say it is, you have the green light to use the four-wheeler whenever you like."

We saddled up Cheveyo and Chase and headed out, winding our way up the ridge where we could follow the fence line. Just as he said that there were no weak areas, the cattle were grazing quietly, and all looked in order.

We went back towards the barn, after the horses were cared for, and I invited Brandon to help me with something. "Take a ride with me out to check the hay fields. I planted them last year in hopes of baling hay and selling it to generate an income for the ranch as well as cut down on the feed expenses."

We had had a pretty good year so far weather-wise, so the hay looked lush. "I should think we may be able to get a few bales by fall when most people are getting their fourth cutting." I told him, "You can get off early today, and I will do the evening feeding."

He insisted on staying to help.

Later after supper, Anna and I were in the den relaxing, and she asked me, "Why did you really enter the room upstairs?"

I firmly told her, "I told you earlier; I heard something in there!"

She pressed me harder saying, "I think it was curiosity and nothing more."

I had to give in and tell her the truth. "I am curious as to what mystery lies in the fate of this ranch. Nobody seems to know what really happened to Ole' man Ames, or why he lost the ranch. It was one of the most successful cattle ranches in the area. I thought the locked room held a clue. "

Anna said, "All I know was his daughter died in a car accident when the creek flooded, and her car was swept away; she was around twenty-one or twenty-two at the time.

"Silas adored his 'princess' as he called her, and his grief drove him to drink. He let the farm responsibilities go, and then he began saying he saw his daughter, that she was here, that she spoke with him every day. Of course, people thought he was crazy; that he had truly gone off the deep end.

"His sister came from Michigan and tried to talk some sense into him, but in the end, when the bank foreclosed on the ranch, she convinced him the best thing to do was for him to seek help. He was admitted to a facility in Albuquerque. That's all I know, and I learned that from Sadie; she seems to know all the area gossip. Maybe you should ask her if she has any other info," Anna suggested. She added, "Why do you want to know so badly?"

I answered, "I wanted to find out where the owner was so I could talk with him about the spread. I actually want to try and buy it from the bank, but I would like to ask Silas what made it so successful before the fall, so I don't repeat his mistakes."

Anna said, "Oh, that makes sense, I guess."

I pleaded, "Anna don't you get it? I want to buy it so we can stay here together, you, and me, forever."

Anna looked forlorn, she said, "I do get it, but I do not know how we could make it work."

"You let me worry about that little darlin'!" I gave her a kiss on her forehead and suggested they head to bed.

She giggled saying, "That would be wonderful."

Last night's dream was back to normal . . . Anna was splendid; her curves were silhouetted in the moonlight as she walked across the ridge to lie down on the blanket, I lay on top of her and covered her as she arched her back. I began to thrust, and she started to buck wildly beneath me, clutching me to her so tightly I could feel her nails diggin' into my back. Our movements escalated until we succumbed and climaxed together. I tumbled off her feelin' spent and luxuriated in the thrill of the aftershocks electrifying my body.

She murmured somethin' unintelligible, and we stared at the sky in our intoxicated state, completely silent and at ease in the world.

I felt the sunbeams warm on my skin and decided it was time to haul myself up and out of this bed. I glanced over at Anna still snuggled beneath the covers with a serene look on her face, and could not find the heart to disturb her, so I quietly slipped out of the room and into the kitchen.

I found Brandon in the kitchen, having his second helping of eggs and bacon. He has made himself right at home now, no longer waiting to be invited in for breakfast. I certainly couldn't complain as he saw to the horses before he came in to eat. He had been a blessing here on the ranch. He said, "I want to know if you would like to go with me and my mom on Sunday to tour the ruins and have her explain the pictographs in more detail."

"I would love to; I will have to check with Anna as she may enjoy getting out also."

"Sure, bring her along!"

Our day was uneventful except for the fox sneaking off with

an egg in his mouth. I asked Brandon, "Can you secure the hen enclosure? We don't need to share any more of our breakfast with that ole' fox." He went to do that before shutting up the barn.

"Can I stay for supper? My mom has plans after work. Her tour group invited her to Santa Fe to eat at the Cowgirl Café."

I said, "Sure, it would be my pleasure for you to join us; your mom didn't invite you along?"

"Oh, she did; it is just that. I still had work to do here and I get bored talking to a bunch of strangers. Answering their silly questions, I would much rather be here with you." I felt endeared by that statement and felt his heart melt just a little.

Dinner was waiting for us in the kitchen. Sadie had left homemade bean soup and cornbread with sour cream and cheese as the fixin's. We dug in as we worked hard today and did not stop for breakfast.

Anna asked Brandon, "Where is your mom tonight?"

He had to explain it again to her about the invite.

She then asked him about school and his plans for college after he graduated in a couple of years.

"I have this great love for ancient cultures, and I want to apply to the University of Texas in Austin, as they have one of the best programs for anthropology at the College of Liberal Arts."

Anna commended him on his certainty for the future. She said, "When I was your age, all I was worried about was riding my horse and winning ribbons at the county fair!"

Brandon assured her, "I also love my horse" and asked about her horse she had when she was a child.

She said, "My horse was named Jorge, and he was my best friend."

"There is a horse here named George, too."

"I know, just like my childhood horse, and that is why I like to ride him and why I call him Jorge instead of George," Anna added. "Although Jorge's registered name was Tijuana Cabin; he was by Cabin Bar Command and out of Tijuana Jewel, Tijuana George was not available when I applied to the AQHA for his name. They assigned a Tijuana Cabin to him. I still liked to call him Jorge as I was not fond of either of those monikers."

"My horse is a Rez pony, but it doesn't matter to me if he has papers or not; he is the best horse, and his name means 'Spirit Warrior,' and that is what he is!" Brandon helped clean up the table and said, "I will be heading home now as tomorrow is another workday, but at least it is Friday!"

They said goodnight, and Ma'ii headed home.

Anna told him, "Drive safely."

I asked, "Would you like to share a bottle of wine? I found a nice Shiraz from an Arizona winery in Jerome, called Passion Cellars."

She said, "I feel a bit of a headache coming on, but you

should enjoy it."

"Hey Anna, would like to go with me to Jerome one day? It is a lovely, little, abandoned mining town and it has a history of being haunted. They even have ghost tours we can go on. There is the best bed and breakfast ever up on the hill; we could stay in the romantic carriage house."

"Maybe one day, that would be nice." I thought her response lacked enthusiasm though. But with her, everything was baby steps.

I said, "Speaking of getting out, Brandon asked if we would like to join him and his mom at the ruins, so she could interpret the pictographs for us and share a bit more of the history. It is normally closed on Sunday, so it will just be the four of us, and we can have a picnic there."

Anna agreed, "That does sound like fun."

I lit the fire and opened the wine. It felt good to just sit and enjoy the peace and quiet. No noise except for the popping and crackling of the fire. The wine was flavorful. It had a hint of lavender. It was also spicy and oaky. It had a smooth finish, and I loved the bottle.

They would customize it with your birth month label. Mine was a lion as I was a Leo born on July twenty-eighth. *Anna's birthday is November fourth, a Scorpio, which is why she sizzles in bed,* I thought.

I dozed off and woke much later to find I was alone in the den; I crept upstairs and slid into bed as not to awaken her. Tonight was dreamless; I attributed that to the wine. Apparently, it creates impotence in dreams as well as in the physical world.

The weekend flew by and it was soon time to head to the ruins with Tori and Brandon. I packed up their lunch and threw the bottle of wine in as it still was three fourths full. Tori picked them up in her cute little Jeep, and off they went to the ruins.

"San Cristobal," Anna giggled as she loved the way that word rolled off of the tongue.

Tori is quite knowledgeable about the pictographs. She explained the difference between pictographs and petroglyphs. "Pictographs are painted, and petroglyphs are carved or pecked into the stone face," She explained, "We are in the basin, and it is considered the Southern Tewa Province and the petroglyphs we are now looking at, are in the classic Rio Grande style." She went on to explain that many of the rock art in this area depicts warfare, but the San Cristobal site is different in that they used the rocks for their buildings. "There is also a convent here and rock art on the adjacent boulder field and cliffs. This pueblo sits on the banks of the Arroyo San Cristobal, which is a permanent water source. The rock art on the cliffs and in the boulder field north of the pueblo is extraordinary in its variety, abundance, and diversity. The majority of the panels in this area are Puebloan, but examples from earlier periods—the

Archaic—are also present."

Anna and I were very impressed, and now I knew where Brandon obtained his vast knowledge of the area.

We decided to sit beneath the bluffs with the rock art as our backdrop for lunch. Tori said, "This is world class dining at its finest," and they all laughed, but knew it was true.

Brandon added, "We are in the original 'Hard Rock Café'!"

When Tori saw the bottle of wine, she exclaimed: "This is my favorite wine, and I love Jerome, the artist community, the mystery, the ghosts, the fine food, and of course the wineries." She said, "I have stayed at the Surgeon's House B&B, and it was so lovely with its beautiful Gardens, books, and a very unique and wonderful owner, Anastasia. All of the rooms were quaint, yet I chose the carriage house, as it was like being in a fairytale."

I said, "Wow, me too!" I added, "Just last night I had asked Anna to go visit Jerome with me soon."

Tori looked at Anna, "You should do it; it was memorable, and you could eat at the Haunted Hamburger as it is across the street from the B&B."

Anna just nodded; she really did not like the chemistry between her friend and me.

Tori felt uneasy, she could tell that Anna was upset, most likely about the connection she has with me. Tori would never betray her friend, which is why she was keeping her feelings in check.

She decided to change the subject. I said, "Brandon's birthday is in three weeks, and he would love to celebrate it at the ranch if that is okay with you two?"

Anna exclaimed, "I love parties! I would love to help in any way I can." She told Tori, "I have a knack for flower arranging and party planning."

Tori said, "Well, then it is settled; I will leave the planning and décor to you, thank you, Anna. Luckily Sept 11th fell on a Saturday this year."

Brandon said, "I really don't have any friends that I want to invite, but I would like it to be just family, which you two, Seth and Anna, are a part of."

We agreed to keep it to the "family" then.

I asked, "What about Brandon's father? Should we invite him?" All Tori would say is, "He passed away. It is just the two of us."

We finished the tour of the ruins and packed up the Jeep. It was sunset and the sky had streaks of pink, orange, and purple slashing through it. It was as if God had picked up a paintbrush and made streaks of watercolors in the vast blue sky. They all agreed that they never tired of the sunsets, or the stars. Tori climbed in behind the wheel and the rest followed suit.

I was excited about the party and wondered what I could do that would be special for the boy. I remembered that the PRCA rodeo was being held at Tingley Coliseum and Arena in September.

It was on September 13th and I had a good friend who was working as a pick-up man in it, my friend Dillon. I knew Dillon could get me and Brandon in behind the chute gates so he could mingle with the Cowboys; it would be perfect! I placed the call to Dillon.

Dillon said, "It is no problem, J bar J were supplying the stock and the owner Zane is a close friend; he may even let Brandon help out. I will arrange V.I.P. passes to be at will call for pick up on the 13th of September.

I thanked my friend and hung up. I could not wait to wrap up a box with a note inside explaining the gift. That way Brandon had something to open on his actual Birthday. He was going to be surprised for sure.

I asked Anna, "Could you do a rodeo theme for the party?" She, of course, wanted to know why, so I explained about the surprise.

"The boy will love it!" Anna agreed. "That will be an easy theme to accomplish."

"I would like to grill steaks and have all the fixin's to go with them."

"Okay, I will make a list and next time you run into Santa Fe you can pick up the supplies I will need."

I thought I could probably get live music too. I would work on that soon.

The next day Anna was in a bit of a foul mood.

I inquired, "Why is my normally sunny Anna feeling so gloomy?"

She just said, "Nothing's wrong."

I knew when a woman said 'nothing's wrong' that something was definitely wrong. I said, "Come on Anna, spill it."

She snapped, "I like having a friend, yet the time you devote to Brandon and Tori makes me a bit jealous."

I retorted, "THIS again? Anna, I am in love with you; I live with you! I have grown close to Brandon, and I have enough love to share. You are my special girl, and you know it!"

She said, "I know I should not be jealous of Tori, but you and she have so much in common and I can see the chemistry between you."

"I cannot help that we have a lot in common, and if I am truthful I have to admit she is a beautiful woman, but my heart is yours, and I will remain true to you." I actually at that moment decided to get down on one knee and propose to her.

When I dropped to my knee, Anna exclaimed, "WHAT ON EARTH ARE YOU DOING? I, get up!"

"No! Anna Jones, will you marry me?"

She said teasingly "I will have to think about it . . ."

"WHAT?"

"Of course, I will marry you!" Now she had two parties to plan, the birthday, and the wedding, HER wedding. She realized too late that this most likely could not happen because of her circumstances, but she could dream and plan none the less. She could not wait to tell Tori. She would ask her to be her maid of honor.

I thought to myself, *What did I do?* I was not in a position to afford a wife or a ring! I let my emotions get the better of me. Well, maybe we would have to have a long engagement.

The next week consisted of a lot of work; I had to get all of the baling equipment ready to bale the first cut of the hay I planted ... it would not be the best crop since my first cutting was happening when everyone else was on their fourth, but suitable for the cattle and next year I could sell the second and third cuttings, keeping the first and fourth for the ranch. I had to go into Albuquerque to get bailing twine for the bailer and a few parts that I couldn't get in Santa Fe. I thought I may do some more snooping around while I was there.

I asked Ma'ii, "Can you handle the chores alone today? You can use the four-wheeler to check the fences and the herd." I explained further, "I have to go into Albuquerque and will be late getting back so you can take off when everything is finished, and Sadie will have lunch for you when you are ready to eat." I waved as he drove out of the driveway.

When I got to Albuquerque, I went straight to the Tractor and Farm Store, but much to my dismay they did not have what I needed.

The parts department sent me to the New Holland Supply

Store in Belen, N.M. It was about thirty-five minutes south of Albuquerque. It was going to be a long day. I plugged the address for Valley Tractor into his GPS and headed down to Belen.

After I got what I needed, I decided to stop in at the library and see what I could find out about the facility Silas was in. No luck there, so far Sadie was the only source of information I had. I might ask her if she knew the name of the facility.

I also had to stop by the bank and inquire on how much the note for the ranch was and see if they could work with me on the purchase. As I approached the bank, I saw a bookstore next door, so I popped in and the first thing I saw was a book of poetry, it was *Unseen Rains, Quatrains of RUMI* by John Moyne and Coleman Barks. I knew I had to get that for Anna; how surprised she would be!

I waited nervously for the bank manager to come and get me for their meeting. The head financial officer of the bank came out to meet me; he introduced myself as Harvey P. Wentworth the III. Harvey escorted me back to his plush office. We took our seats and Harvey asked me, "How can I be of service?"

I replied, "I am interested in purchasing the Ames property. I am currently the acting caretaker for the spread."

Harvey said, "I knew you came in about Silas's ranch, but that was not what I was expecting to hear from you. I thought perhaps you needed a larger allowance for equipment, feed, and such."

I replied, "The current allowance has been covering expenses, and I planted the hay fields to generate income," to which, Harvey looked impressed.

I asked him, "Can you please explain the process of buying a foreclosed property, what all it entails?"

Harvey began, "That is a mighty large spread for a first-time buyer."

I said confidently, "My brother is pretty well off, and I was thinkin' about askin' him to be an investor in the venture."

"I see," said Harvey. "Well, okay, Son, there are two types of foreclosures: judicial and non-judicial. This foreclosure was handled judiciously: which means that Silas's lawyer was involved in the proceedings.

"Back when Silas bought the ranch, he paid around 2.8 million and the remaining amount with a loan, which puts a value of the property at around 8 million today, but that is irrelevant when purchasing a foreclosure. We just need to recoup the remainder of the loan. He had borrowed another million for stock and equipment etc. The ranch was doing very well for the last couple of decades, and Silas came from money.

"His family has a trust for Anna, which he refused to use, as he could have paid off the note by liquidating that. He also has investments that could have been liquidated and used, yet in his state of mind, he was unable to make sound business decisions. Furthermore, he told us to just take it as it, the ranch, no longer held meaning for him without Anna. He is a close personal friend of mine after all; I tried to find a way around this mess.

"So, the note stands at around $500,000.00. As you know business goes up and down, so sometimes he would ask to extend the loan a bit. Other times he would pay large chunks off. Son, do you think you could come up with that kind of money? Plus, would you have the money to run the ranch?"

I said, "Well, I hope so, as it sounds like a great investment to me! Paying five hundred thousand for a ranch that is worth eight million, how could I go wrong?"

Harvey explained, "There are also the taxes; we paid them up to date, and you will have closing costs. Taxes are based on $7,334.00 an acre for half the spread and $4,500.00 an acre for the other half as it is unimproved pastureland. Although you do have deductions for feed, equipment, livestock transport, etc."

I could not conceal my excitement as I said, "My brother is a number cruncher, so he could handle the books with no problem. What were the taxes last year?"

"I will have to look at the assessor's papers. Just hold on a minute." He rifled through the papers on his desk, "They were around $25,000.00 last year."

"Woo wee," I replied.

Harvey cautioned, "It is quite a financial responsibility you are asking to take on, why don't you just sleep on it a while and see if you still want to embark on this venture."

I said, "Thank you, Sir, for your time, and there is one more thing you can help me with . . ."

"What would that be son?"

"You said you are close with Silas, and I wanted to talk to him about the Ranch. Could you tell me where he is living now?"

Harvey looked hesitant, but finally decided to tell me the name of the facility, "It is the Sage Rehabilitation and Care Center right here in Albuquerque. It is on Jefferson."

I thanked him again for his time and the information saying, "I hope to be back soon and seal the deal."

Harvey suggested that I speak with Silas's lawyer as well, and he gave me the name, "Talbert Haskins, he is located right here in Albuquerque."

I said, "I can't thank you enough" and headed out the door.

It had been a very long day and I did not have time to stop for a visit with Silas today. I probably should call first anyway, as those types of places normally had visiting hours with rules and regulations. I started up the truck and headed home. My brain was on overload, and I needed to be in the barn with the horses and Anna to unwind; maybe she was up for an evening ride I thought. I gave her a call . . .She answered and said, "Hello", but there was so much static I had to ask her to yell to be heard.

I finally said, "I am on my way see you soon and hung up."

I pulled into the drive with a cloud of dust in his trail. I was going a bit faster than I should for the stone driveway in my hurry to be home, and the truck tires spun a bit and it fishtailed as I sped up the lane.

I saw Anna in her garden and came to a stop by the house. I hollered at her, and she ran to meet me. She said, "you were gone a long time today baby."

"I know! I had to drive to the south end of Albuquerque to find the part for the bailer and then I stopped by the bank; I have something I want to run by you."

"What is it?"

I explained my plan to buy the ranch, and she looked skeptical. "Well that is a lot of money, how would we afford the upkeep?" she inquired.

"Let me worry about that. I do not want you to stress your pretty little head about such things because that is the man's job."

"OH, Seth!"

Anna showed me my supper and suggested a cold beer; afterward, we headed to the barn and saddled up for our evening ride. I asked her, "How did Brandon do today? Being on his own?"

"Oh, he did a great job as far as I can tell, but he sure does eat a lot! Sadie teased him that he was eating her out of house and home."

I said, "Well, he is a growing boy! At least feeding him is cheaper than paying the going rate for a Ranch Hand."

She had to agree with that. We settled into a familiar silence, and I enjoyed the cool breeze settling across the ridge. We stopped to watch the sunset, staying mounted on the horses, then headed home. After today I was definitely ready for one of my Galisteo nights.

Just as I had hoped Anna came to me in my sleep: slowing peeling away his layers of clothing and stress, with each kiss I felt a bit more relaxed until she reached my groin area; then I felt the strain of excitement and the need for release. My desire for her was so strong that I pulled her off of me and rolled her onto her back. I ached for her and overwhelmed her with my hard penetration. She gasped. I asked if me had hurt her and she replied softly, "No, please keep going, harder baby . . ." Her wish was my command. The heat flared with every thrust until I felt as if I was pounding her. She arched and met my every move just as fiercely! Soon we were immersed in the throes of orgasm and then lay sated in one another's arms.

CHAPTER THREE

When I got up Friday morning, I came down to the kitchen early and when I caught Sadie alone, I began asking her questions. Brandon was out in the barn and Anna was still upstairs. Sadie loved to gossip, and she could not wait to tell me about the downward spiral of the ranch owner.

She began with the car accident, what she added to the story was . . . "Anna had fallen in love with one of the Ranch hands, but one evening as a storm was coming in, she ran down to the barn to check on her beloved Jorge. She heard moans coming from the tack room, curious she looked inside and found her love having relations with another woman; (yes, she actually used the word relations!)

"Anna flew into a rage when she saw them together. Her

lover, Gabriel, was behind this blond bimbo, what she called a buckle bunny from the rodeo circuit, and he was thrusting himself into her as she bent over Anna's saddle! She hit Gabo, as she called him, over the head with the handle of the rake that was near the door. As he grabbed his head saying, 'What the Hell?' blood ran through his fingers dripping down his face. Anna spun and grabbed the girl by her hair, dragging her out into the barn aisle where she kicked her several times, or so the story goes . . .," said Sadie.

"Gabo came out and shoved Anna off of the girl and Anna ran to her car just as the rain began to fall, it was a deluge, and the creek began to rise swiftly. Anna drove off into the night heading towards U.S. 285; by the time she hit the bridge over Galisteo Creek, the water was over the road and her car was picked up and began to spin. It bounced off of a boulder and got wedged upside down. The water was still rising, and she was trapped.

"Her father heard the ruckus at the barn on the security monitor. By the time he reached the barn, Anna was gone and Gabo and the girl were gathering their things to go. Silas asked what happened, and before Gabo could finish the first sentence, well, Silas began to beat the living daylights out of him; he almost killed him, and if the girl hadn't called the police, he probably would have!"

Before she continued her story, she took a breath, "Silas jumped into his pickup and took off in search of Anna. Gabo and the girl left. They lit outta these parts; no one has seen 'em since. Silas had called the police himself to report Anna missing.

"When he reached U.S. 285, there was a blockade, not only because of the flash flooding but because there was a car underwater and a rescue team was working to free the woman inside. Silas knew it was his 'Princess,' and he ran past the blockade trying to get to her, but the officers held him back.

"When they pulled her from the wreckage, he saw his worst fears were realized. Anna was lifeless, and they put her on a stretcher as they worked on her, trying to revive her. They had to take her to Santa Fe in an ambulance. Silas followed behind them, but she was pronounced dead on arrival at the hospital."

Just then Brandon came into the kitchen, and I made a motion to Sadie to be quiet. The rest of the story could wait.

As he handed Sadie a basket full of eggs, Brandon reported, "The chicken coop stayed safe last night."

She said, "Thank you, sweetie."

And then she addressed both men, "Breakfast was already made today; y'all are having oatmeal with fruit and toast, but I will make eggs tomorrow."

They sat down to eat just as Anna entered the kitchen. Brandon thought it was odd that Sadie never greeted Anna, or that he had never heard them have a conversation. He thought he would ask me about it later as it would be rude to confront Anna or Sadie.

Brandon and I were in the barn saddling the horses for the

day's work when Ma'ii said to me, "Seth, I have a question for you?"

"Shoot," I replied.

"How come Sadie and Anna never talk?"

I pondered that a minute and said, "I don't really know. I guess they just feel comfortable in one another's company."

Brandon thought there was more to it than that; he has had his suspicions for a while now, but he did not want to get on my bad side, so he just said, "Oh, that is nice."

I thought to myself that I was not the only one that thought it odd then. I was going to have to come up with a way to ask Anna about it without offending her. It was the last thing on my mind later on though, when I was elbow deep in tractor grease getting all the equipment ready for bailing tomorrow.

I asked Brandon, "Are you ready for bailing?"

Brandon replied, "Sure am!"

I said, "I will need you Sunday as well so we can get it all done by Wednesday, as there is rain predicted. May not come to pass, but wet hay will not do us any good."

"Sure, I am up for it, and maybe Mom would come and visit Anna while we work."

"Sounds like a plan!" I said, "Now, can you hand me that wrench?"

We worked late that day, and Ma'ii asked if he could stay for dinner again, "Of course" was my reply.

When we got in the pickup to head to the house, Ma'ii almost sat on the bag with the poetry book in it. "What's this?"

I said, "I forgot about it in my haste to get in the house last night; it is a gift for Anna."

Ma'ii asked, "May I look at it as I also love poetry; one of my favorite poems is 'My Law' By Blavatsky."

I whistled, "That sure is some heavy reading material for a young man; I did not read Blavatsky until I was in my second year at Yale!"

Ma'ii explained to him, "Things come to me in a dream state, and this poem came to me one night when I was just twelve. I had gone to a sweat lodge to meditate on it, and that is where the author's name was revealed to me. I went to the library and looked her up. It was such a wonderful philosophy, and it got me interested in reading more of the Theosophical texts.

"I now am reading Rudolph Steiner's book on Anthroposophical Medicine. He uses plants extensively to cure ailments; one of his controversial uses of mistletoe is to cure cancer. As a Native American, the earth and four elements are sacred, so, I can relate. He also was the pioneer of biodynamic agriculture and the Waldorf school system.

"That is where my mother sent me as she does not like the archaic school system which is used in this country today. She explained to me that our ancestors, her grandparents, were taken from their family and put into 'English' schools. The 'Whiteman's Language' was all they were allowed to speak; they tried to eradicate our heritage and wisdom with colonization. I decided to learn as much as possible about natural ways and Steiner is a leader in this area. I also love the writings of White Eagle for spiritual studies."

I was highly impressed by this young man, and I told him so. "If I ever have children, I will send them to the Waldorf School for sure. Brandon do you know the poem My Law by heart?"

"I surely do!"

"Would you recite it for Anna? She would love it!"

When we entered the kitchen, Anna was at the table waiting.

After we ate, I handed her the surprise. She was so excited she was nearly bursting at the seams with joy. I said, "We have another surprise for you: Brandon is also fond of poetry and he would like to recite his favorite poem to you. She looked expectantly at Brandon and he began:

MY LAW

The sun may be coloured, yet ever the sun

Will sweep on its course till the Cycle is run.

And when into chaos the system is hurled

Again shall the Builder reshape a new world.

Your path may be clouded, uncertain in your goal:

Move on – for your orbit is fixed to your soul.

And though it may lead into darkness of night
The torch of the Builder shall give it new light.
You were. You will be! Know this while you are:
Your spirit has travelled both long and afar.
It came from the Source, to the Source it returns –
The Spark which was lighted eternally burns.
It slept in a jewel. It leapt in a wave.
It roamed in the forest. It rose from the grave.
It took on strange garbs for long eons of years
And now in the soul of yourself It appears.
From body to body your spirit speeds on
It seeks a new form when the old one has gone
And the form that it finds is the fabric you wrought
On the loom of the Mind from the fibre of Thought.
As dew is drawn upwards, in rain to descend
Your thoughts drift away and in Destiny blend.
You cannot escape them, for petty or great,
Or evil or noble, they fashion your Fate.
Somewhere on some planet, sometime and somehow
You will reflect your thoughts of your Now.
My Law is unerring, no blood can atone –
The structure you built you will live in – alone.
Your lives with your longings will ever keep pace
And all that you ask for, and all you desire

Must come at your bidding, as flame out of fire.
Once list' to that Voice and all tumult is done –
Your life is the life of the Infinite One.
In the hurrying race you are conscious of pause
With love for the purpose, and love for the Cause.
You are your own Devil, you are your own God
You fashioned the paths your footsteps have trod.
And no one can save you from Error or Sin
Until you have hark'd to the Spirit within.

After reciting, he analyzed, "This poem is based on Theosophy, and it was written by Madame Helena Petrova Blavatsky, and I learned about her in a dream. For me, this poem sums up life and gives it meaning; a purpose. It is the formula for becoming a person who will do good in the world and contribute to making it a better place; it also comforts me to know that we are eternal, our spirit lives on."

Anna said, "It is very deep for such a young man; I am truly impressed by your wisdom."

He explained his mother's choice of schooling for him. "I have been blessed with an education at the Santa Fe Waldorf School and a rich heritage from my ancestors; the spirit world is sacred, and this poem blends that world with the material world."

I piped in, "I would love to educate my children at the

Waldorf School . . ."

At this Anna's eyes flashed angrily, and she left the room.

Ma'ii asked, "What just happened?"

I frowned, "I forgot that Anna cannot have children and what I just said was insensitive, especially because I have asked her to marry me."

Brandon asserted, "You better go fix this now! I should head home; I never like leaving mom alone in the evenings." He headed out to the four-wheeler, and I went upstairs to sooth Anna's emotions.

"Anna, honey, I am sorry that I was insensitive to your feelings; I simply forgot."

"YOU FORGOT!" A vase from the dresser where Anna stood flew at my head!

"ANNA! What has gotten into you lately? Where is the sweet woman I fell in love with?"

She began to sob and turned to him saying, "She is right in front of you, but it seems that you no longer want her!"

"Oh Anna, that simply is not true; I love you," I dropped my head into my hands. "I wasn't thinking when I blurted that out; it was a normal thought for an unmarried man ---"

She retorted, "Now, you are making it worse!"

"I am going to go to the barn to let my feelings settle down; I suggest you go to your garden or for a walk so your emotions can

simmer down, and later we can speak to one another like adults."
With that, I spun around and walked out.

Anna observed, *He isn't just walking out of the room; he is
walking away from me.*

I was rattled and needed to clear my head. Yes, what I said
was insensitive, but I wanted always wanted kids, yet, I fell in love
with Anna, so I chose her and decided to put my dream of having a
bunch of little Seth's running around in the back of my mind. I should
not have been so careless as to just blurt that out. Maybe I really
should explore my feelings; I should not marry Anna if I am going to
resent her for not being able to give me a child.

I saddled up Chase and headed for the backcountry. *A nice
long ride in the high desert is always good for the heart and soul.
Nature is certainly a healer; at least it is for me.* I found myself at the
San Cristobal ruins. I tied Chase up in the shade and decided to take
a walk and look at the drawings on the bluff. I began examining the
strange art: I saw a symbol that looked like a dog and above it was
one with alien eyes and an open mouth with teeth; below that was
a face with a tail off to the side wearing a grimace as if the dog had
eaten its body. There were three stars inside the dog . . . I was lost
in thought, *What could these symbols mean, do they have meaning,
or are they just doodles?* The more I looked at it, the more I saw,
there were many stars and other galactic symbols, possibly it was
the milky way and star constellations. The art seemed to speak of

life beyond this world. It did resemble a spirit realm, or, as Ma'ii called it, the outer limits of the cosmos.

At that moment I heard a sound that brought me back to this earth. I turned to see what it was, and saw Tori exiting a tour van with a group of people. She approached me, "What a nice surprise to see you out here."

"Yeah, you too. I normally don't come out here this late but can explain later. Ummm, why are you bringing a tour group out this late in the evening?"

"Once a month we do a full moon tour and tonight is the night of the full moon, so here we are! You can stay for the tour if you'd like. and I will talk with you after I get my folks back on the tour bus headed home. You look like you could use a friendly ear."

"Thank you, it would be my pleasure."

I listened to Tori tell about the myths and the research that has been done on the rock art. She was explaining, "The faces without bodies were masks; some were horned, and some had their mouth open. Others looked fierce; some of them were thought to be arrow eaters, the ones with horns, and others are thought to be animal priests. The Bear is normally a symbol of war, yet, this bear appears to be in the cosmos and most likely is a representation of the constellation Ursa Major. Some of the other figures in this panel may represent beings or medicine men, suggesting that this is about spirituality and the study of the stars, cosmetology."

She moved on to another panel with what looked like two snakes and an eagle. She explained, "This panel is a depiction from the Puebloan people; to them the eagle symbolizes the spirit of the deity of 'above' while the serpent represents the spirit of the deity of 'below.' This is a representation of a complex illustration of the interplay of the powers of above and below leading to balance in the world."

She went on to point out depictions of corn and other agricultural drawings and concluded with her moonwalk imitation, which made everyone laugh.

She addressed the group, "Well, this completes the full moon tour; it wouldn't be complete without a 'moonwalk'!"

I gazed at Tori and thought her vast knowledge and uniqueness amazed me. I could listen to her speak all night long. This was another reason I am having second thoughts about marrying Anna.

Everyone headed to the tour van. Tori looked at me and asked, "Can you take me to my car at the train station?"

I had to tell her I was without a vehicle as well. "I am here on horseback, and isn't it about an hour drive to the train station in Lamay?"

"Yes, it is! How about you wait for me here, and I will return."

"It is late, and I must get back as I am on horseback. I did not have a flashlight because every time I go to use one, the batteries are dead; in fact, all the batteries in the house are dead. I attribute it to them being old." I alluded to trouble between me and Anna, adding, "I would like to talk to you about that, you know a female perspective. How about lunch tomorrow?"

"Yeah, that would be great. I have a break from two until three-thirty."

"Alrighty, Ma'am, I shall meet you here, the same place tomorrow. I will even bring a lunch, specially made by Sadie!" I tipped his hat and watched her get into the van and drive away. I best be getting back, the moon was rising in the sky and he did not want to be out past dark-- or face more of Anna's rage.

I contemplated his situation as I rode home. I did love Anna, but something was happening to her; she was changing. Maybe it was the full moon, or maybe something else. The only way to fix it was to talk to her about it. The stars began to pop out just as I reached the barn; I brushed Chase down and gave all three of the horses a carrot as a treat and then headed to the house.

Anna heard him come in, and, instead of greeting me, lit into me again, "WHERE HAVE YOU BEEN? I was worried!"

I said, "Anna, please, can we talk about this calmly?"

"NO!" she spat and then stormed off to bed.

Looks like it is the couch for me tonight!

I washed up and lay down to rest. I had a nice cool beer from the fridge, and I turned on the sports channel for Rodeo. I rarely watched television, but I wanted to get out of my head and rest my body and my brain. I dozed off and had a dream, but this was another dream about Tori and Brandon; they were all at the ruins having a picnic and laughing, they were a family. I awoke with a longing I had not felt before. I decided that Anna and I had to talk . . . . I would see how she felt in the morning. I turned over and went back to sleep.

I awoke in the morning with the T.V. still on and a kink in my back which did nothing to improve my mood.

I headed into the kitchen just as Sadie arrived. I asked her, "Can you discreetly pack a picnic lunch for two?"

She raised an eyebrow at me, "Sure thing boss."

I went to splash water on my face and see if Anna was up. I tried my bedroom door, but to my dismay, it was locked. *Well, I would just wait her out.* I went back to the kitchen and poured a cup of coffee; Brandon came in and sat down with me. We talked about bailing today while Sadie cooked omelets for them.

He told Ma'ii, "There is somewhere I have to be at two in the afternoon, so we will take a two-hour break from bailing and that will give you time to eat lunch and clean the stalls."

Ma'ii asked, "Where are you going"?

"To run an errand."

After breakfast they went to the barn. I told Brandon, "You

can let the horses out to graze in the front pasture as we won't be using them for the next couple of days."

We bailed for the next five hours in the blazing sun.

I said, "I have to go now."

Ma'ii was thankful for the break, the sun was like fire today! I loaded the picnic basket in the truck and waved as I drove down the lane. Ma'ii thought it odd that I had a picnic basket for running errands.

I arrived at the ruins site just a few minutes before Tori. I got out of his truck as she drove in. We hugged and walked to the shaded area where there were a few picnic tables.

"It is really good to see you, Seth. So, what did you want to talk about?"

I began with the fight that Anna and I had last night. I admitted, "Yes, I was insensitive, yet, I feel she overreacted to it. Actually, she has been in a mood since I met you; she has become jealous and moody; questioning everything I do.

"I am sorry to hear that; I mean no trouble."

I assured her, "You have done nothing wrong. As long as I am bein' honest, I am catching a few feelings toward you, Tori."

She just said, "Oh."

"I don't mean to make you feel uncomfortable."

"It's okay; I don't." As long as we are being honest, I have been feeling the same towards you."

"Well, this is a predicament for sure, as we both care about Anna."

She agreed. They began to eat, and both were silent for a few minutes.

After Tori finished her lunch, she said, "Maybe I should stay away for a while."

I looked up at her, "That is not the answer. I explained that I have asked Anna to marry him, and she was planning to ask you to be her maid of honor, as you are her only friend."

Tori was taken aback by that revelation. "This is going to make that a bit awkward for me, Seth."

"I know. I am not sure it is the right thing to do now as she has changed completely from the sweet woman I fell in love with, and I really want a family. I don't know if she told you or not, but she is unable to have children." I took a breath and asked, "Tori, can you help me decide what to do?"

She said, "Well, I cannot speak for another person, but while you guys are bailing hay tomorrow, I can talk to her if you like; she may open up to another woman."

"I would love that and, Tori, I am sorry for creating this awkwardness between us."

"There is nothing we can do about it. We can't help whom we are attracted to; at least, we have integrity and are keeping ourselves in check."

They were cleaning up to leave and she said, "Seth, I need to share something with you."

He looked up, "Shoot."

She explained to him she came from a long line of seers; that she had medicine woman powers, and she thought that Brandon had them, too. "Brandon and I both have a strong connection to the spirit world and are able to see those souls that have passed on. I believe unsettled spirits get stuck on this earth and, at times, become angry; they may even take possession of another person to stay here and experience things."

She was quiet for a moment and when I did not respond, she continued, "I have a feeling about Anna . . . I am not sure how Anna would handle it if I asked her about it."

I confided, "This is foreign to me. I have never discussed these types of things with Anna; I cannot say what her beliefs are."

"I will feel her out, broach the subject slowly with her."

I questioned, "Do you think she is a ghost?"

"Well, no, I am not sure yet, but maybe a ghost is affecting her," Torri looked skeptical, "I feel the other Anna is still here and influencing your Anna; after all, her daddy said he saw her, and that is one reason he is in long-term mental health care."

I thanked her with a kiss on the cheek and we went our separate ways.

When I got back to the barn, Anna was there. "Where have

you been?"

"I see you are still sulking; I was running errands."

Brandon was busying himself in the tack room, pretending not to hear them. At that last comment, Anna flew into a rage stomping off, and as she passed the truck, she glanced in and saw the picnic basket. "I demand to know why there is a picnic basket in the truck."

"Anna, you need to calm down."

She did anything but calm down. "You have another woman! I knew IT!"

"NO, Anna, I do not!"

"I do not believe you!" Anna spun and ran toward the house.

Brandon stuck his head out, "Seth, is everything okay?"

"No, it is not, as you can see, but we still have a lot of work to do; let's get going."

They worked late; I finally told Ma'ii, "Let's stop and begin again tomorrow; I am exhausted."

Ma'ii sighed in relief, "Thank goodness! I thought you were going to have us work all night!"

I apologized, "I am just trying to work off my frustration."

"I hope you guys work it out before tomorrow; I don't think I have another day like today in me!"

They both laughed and said, "Goodnight."

Brandon reminded me, "My mom is coming tomorrow, so maybe she can talk to Anna." He added, "Girl talk, ya know?"

"Yes, I know, and I hope so."

Brandon arrived home and told his mother about the fight he witnessed. "Mom, it made me uncomfortable, and maybe you can talk to Anna."

"Sure, Son, I planned on it; she has been different lately."

"I have also sensed something off with Anna."

"You have good intuition. We come from a long line of seers, and I sensed the same thing," She looked at her son. "Right now, you need to get your rest; you look tired, no need to spend energy on this. I will deal with it tomorrow. Sweet Dreams, Mijo."

"I am headed up for a bath. My pillow is calling to me."

His mom said, "Use the medicine salts; they will make your muscles feel better—as well as wash away the negative emotions that you picked up tonight."

He yelled down, "Thanks Mom!"

She was so blessed to have this boy in her life; it made her glad that she did not opt for an abortion. Her beliefs would not allow her to take a life, any life, she believed in all experience being necessary to spiritual growth, even the ones we consider unpleasant; after all, Brandon was born out of one of those unpleasant experiences, and he brought her the greatest joy. She remembered her grandmother telling her to always look for the good, the God, in all things . . . she was a wise woman, and Tori learned a lot from her wisdom. She hoped to pass it down to her son.

I went into the house and Anna was still crying. She was in the den staring out at the moonlit sky. She was singing a song through her tears . . . She crooned, "Fly me home, fly me home, on the wings of an angel, don't ever let go . . ."

I quietly called to her, "Anna." She turned her tear-streaked face toward him, and she looked so lost. "Anna, please forgive me, can we please make up?"

She ran to him, and they embraced. I kissed the top of her hair inhaling the sweet night jasmine scent. "I never meant to hurt you, Hun." She just snuggled closer against his chest.

She asked, "Could you read some of the new poems to me from the Rumi book you gave me?"

"Yes, come on over to the sofa," I sat down and she sat on the sheepskin rug at his feet gazing up at him with her big eyes, her lashes damp. I began . . .

"In the mountains along a creek half-frozen with thick ledges of ice, a friend handed me an icy drop of dew. I held it close to my eye like a lens. The hemlock and the rhododendron and the creek

were suddenly upside down above me! The world reversed in a tear."

I thought, *What an appropriate poem. Whenever a person cried, it was normally because his/her world was turned upside down.* I asked Anna, "Would you like a cup of tea?"

She declined the offer, "No, I just need rest and to be close to you." So, we went upstairs.

I thought how good it felt to be back in the bed beside her. I vowed to myself to be more sensitive with my words and her feelings. I still worried about her moods, but maybe there was more than I knew going on with her. What I did know was that all O could do was to be a support system for her and love her; she would share her feelings if and when she felt the need to. We fell asleep cuddled together like they were one person. Tonight, I had a wonderful dream with Anna as the shining star that she was.

Anna was atop of me straddling me as if I were a horse, facing away from me; she met my upward drive with her downward thrusts. I could see droplets of sweat glowing on her skin, making her look like a diamond with all of her facets shining. I wanted to be immersed deep within her forever. I came up hard as she pushed down onto me. I thought I would break from the strain, and at that moment, I exploded into her softness.

She followed after moaning softly, like the seductress that she was. She fell beside me still sticky from the sweat and the hard work she had done by being on top of him. I thought that there was no woman who could replace her in my life or his dreams. How could I have ever entertained thoughts of being with Tori? *Things of the heart always seem solid in the afterglow of lovemaking; yet, the bright light of day reveals the cracks on the surface.*

CHAPTER FOUR

We had to be up early even though it was Sunday, and it would be another hot one! I groaned as I remembered we still had hay to bale. I whipped up some eggs and sage sausage.

Brandon arrived with Tori and everyone ate their fill. The men left for the hay fields, and the women headed to the garden with a pitcher of iced tea. They sat on the garden chairs with overstuffed cushions covered in a floral pattern.

Anna divulged, "I love flowers so much! I was surrounded by them at . . ."

Tori asked, "At . . .?"

Anna was quiet for a moment and then answered Tori, "At my mother's funeral."

"Oh," responded Tori, "I am sorry you had to suffer through

that experience."

Anna looked perplexed, "That was a rare choice of words."

Tori explained, "I feel that we do not die; we live on . . . as we are made of energy, and it cannot cease to exist. We just change form and move on to another realm. One filled with light and love. Yes, those left behind feel pain and suffering, yet those that transcend are happy."

"I do not feel the same way, and I was sad to have lost my mother when I was just a young girl. My mother drowned when I was around three or four."

Tori empathized, "My own mother had passed away young also, and, whenever I feel that I miss her, I look up at the stars and take in their vastness, knowing my mother is among them looking down at me."

She then confided, "I am able to 'see' spirits, souls, those that have transitioned, or that are stuck here."

Anna asked her, "How did your mother die?"

Tori looked at her hands and took a deep breath, "She was murdered by my stepfather and now he is in prison, and it is a good place for him."

Tori continued, "Spirits that have moved into the light can return to help loved ones on earth, and those with my gift can see and interact with them. Brandon shares my gift. The difference between a spirit and a soul is that a soul is someone who did not enter the light, they are the ones we call ghosts. They normally are stuck here until someone comes along that can help them move into the light or transcend. They often become angry if they are stuck here too long and they may even take possession of a living person's emotional body."

Anna made a strange face, "I do not know if that is true."

Tori had been feeling her out but decided to back off for now. She changed tack. "Anna, I also learned the ways of the medicine woman from my grandmother: Brandon overheard the trouble in the barn the other night, the fight between you and Seth.

"I can help you with your emotions if you'd like; I can perform healing or a series of healings to help release the emotions trapped in the cellular memory, as these create issues in our tissues, so to speak. When we do not get to the root of the issue, it will continue to grow and the root system will become stronger with each growth, each new traumatic experience. It is like your beloved garden, Anna, when you pull the weeds you must make sure they are taken out by the roots, or they return stronger and choke the flowers until they die. It is the same with the human body."

Anna considered, "I will think about it, what you said is a lot to absorb, as it is such a foreign concept to me."

Tori changed the subject again, saying, "I see there is a pool over there; it seems neglected. I love to swim, why isn't it open?"

Anna said, "I do not really know why Seth has kept it closed.

Sadie told me the owner's daughter loved to swim, and ironically, she drowned, and that her father closed the pool up after she passed as he could not bear to look at it. Apparently, it reminded him of her drowning. All that knowledge of swimming did her no good when trapped in a car sinking in the creek."

Tori just said, "Oh."

"I am glad it is closed, as it reminds me of my mother dying also," She added. "Tori, I am glad you are here; I wanted to ask you something."

"Ask away."

Anna gushed, "Seth has asked me to marry him, and I would be honored to have you as my maid of honor."

Tori was glad. Seth had warned her about this so that her face did not register the shock, alerting Anna to her feelings where Seth was concerned. Tori smiled, "It would be my 'honor' to serve as your maid of honor!" They both giggled at the pun and the rest of the afternoon was spent discussing wedding plans.

The boys came in at dusk. I looked to the women, "The last bale has been baled and stored! We are hungry!"

The girls said in unison, "We are too. We have been discussing wedding plans all day and forgot to cook anything . . ." The guys looked shocked. I said, "Ugh! Well, Brandon and I will run into Madrid and grab a few pizzas; can you women at least make a salad while we are gone?"

They started right away on the salad and in no time, we guys returned with the pizza. It was a wood fired pizza from the Holler, they always make great food. We sat down.

Tori asked, "May I say a little prayer before we eat?" She was obliged. "The trees and the grass, all plants have spirits, may we ask forgiveness for taking them in for our necessities, and ask that we are blessed by their nourishment, amen, a'ho."

Everyone dug in. "I am grateful for the short blessing, Mom," Brendan commented. "Sometimes Mom can be long-winded in her gratitude." We all laughed.

The night ended cordially, and I could not get to my bed fast enough. I was going to go to Albuquerque tomorrow and see if I could speak with ole' man Ames. I had called the other day and they told me visiting hours were between noon and five; all I had to do was sign in. I looked forward to findin' out more about the ranch. I figured when I had a solid idea of how it ran, I could share the info with my brother, and we could work on the business plan. I hoped it would be good news and my brother would think it to be a solid investment. Sleep came quickly and I had no dreams that night in my exhausted state.

I helped Brandon with the chores in the morning and asked him, "Would you like to come along to see the ranch owner? You deserve a break after the week we just had!" We set off for Albuquerque.

We arrived at the Sage rehabilitation and Care Center just before one. I signed us in, "We are here to see Silas Ames, err, I need to have a discussion about the ranch with Silas; I am the new caretaker, and this is my ranch hand, Brandon."

The nurse gave him a queer look but led them to a community room where a man she said was Silas sat staring out of the window. "He is right over there, staring out the window."

Brandon and I took seats on either side of Silas. I introduced us to the old man. "I am Seth, and this is Brandon, Sir." Had he not been prepared for the deteriorated state that Silas was in, this may have been a wasted trip.

Silas looked at him, "Do you know My Anna?"

Without thinking as I know Anna, but not Silas's Anna, I blurted, "Yes."

He said excitedly, "Then you see her also; they think I am mad, but she is here, I tell you!" He began to rant and rave. I realized I would get no information from this man with his tortured soul.

Brandon had been silent through the whole ordeal, and I thought that he might have been traumatized, but what Brandon said next shocked him. As they were walking out, he revealed, "I saw her, too. She was faint. I believe that she has attached to him; otherwise, a ghost cannot travel far from their place of death or home. She was there by his side, just as he said, yet, she was faint."

I asked him, "Have you gone mad?"

"No, Seth, I have a gift, just as my mother does; we are seers and we can see spirits and souls that have left this earth plane, or who have chosen to stay."

I felt as if I had stepped into the twilight zone. I said, "Maybe you should stay here with him as I walk toward the exit."

Brandon followed saying, "It is okay to fear that which we do not understand."

I made a face. "Why are you talking like an elder?"

Brandon explained, "It is the respectful way to speak of the old and ancient ways of my peoples and their gifts. It is also out of respect for the spirit world."

"I can't handle this right now."

Brandon suggested, "Maybe you can speak with my mother about this as she is more adept at explaining this aspect of life."

"I will."

When we reached the truck, I spoke again, "Maybe we will have better luck with the lawyer; he handled the foreclosure and was an advisor to Silas. He is sure to know all the business dealings."

I took out the GPS and plugged in the address for Talbert Haskins, Esquire. We arrived twenty minutes later.

I thought it would be good for Brandon to learn the ins and outs of the business, not just the manual labor side of ranching. We entered, and the secretary offered us a seat and some water. She said, "I will let Mr. Haskins know you are here."

She returned a few moments later, "You are in luck as his last client has canceled, and he is free now." She led them through huge, oak, double doors into his office where he sat behind a beautiful mahogany desk.

He motioned to the two chairs in front of his massive desk. "Please have a seat and tell me what I can do for you today."

I explained who I was and the situation at the ranch and about my visit to Silas's care center.

Talbert said, "Yes, it is a sad situation, and Silas has declined in the time that he has been there. He now lives in a world of his own, far removed from the one everyone else inhabits."

I said, "I have been at the ranch for over a year, and I have a fiancé now. I want to have a stable foundation with which to support her. I thought that purchasing the ranch would be a way to build that foundation."

"I see," replied Talbert.

I continued, "Right now, I have a budget from the bank to run the ranch, and I have been keeping under budget since I have taken over the care of the operation. I have also planted hay fields so there will be an income next year to ease the financial burden on the bank. The income from the hay sales will offset the funds needed to run things. I am going to have my brother, a number cruncher, help me write a business plan as soon as I have the information needed about costs and such."

Talbert replied, "I will be happy to show you the spreadsheets for the expenses, etc." He buzzed the secretary and asked her, "Maryanne, please bring me the file for the Ames place?"

She entered a moment later with the file in hand. I thought she sashayed a bit when she walked; maybe it was her tight skirt. I brought my attention back to the business at hand. Talbert went over everything he had with us; Brandon seemed to be absorbing the information like a dry sponge. He offered to have Maryanne copy the file so that I could reference it while making his business plan.

"Thank you for all of your help," I offered as Brandon and I left the office. I swore that Maryanne winked at him on the way out. *Some women*, I thought.

I asked Brandon if there was anything he would like to do while we were in the city. To my surprise, Brandon asked if we could go to old town Albuquerque and eat at a little Navajo place that has amazing fry bread tacos—better known as Indian tacos in these parts. He said, "If you don't mind, I would love to stop at the Natural History Museum after we eat."

I agreed, "You got it; you worked hard last week, and it is my treat."

While we ate their Indian tacos, I asked him, "What is at the History Museum?"

"A movie in the planetarium, it is about fractals. I love this movie and would like to share it with you."

I had to ask, "What is a gosh darn fractal?"

"It is a building block of our DNA, a mathematical fragment."

I crossed my eyes jokingly. "Come again."

Ma'ii laughed, "Let me borrow your phone." He did a Google search and read the explanation to me:

"Fractal, (Frak tel), noun. Plural noun: fractals. A curve or geometric figure, each part of which has the same statistical character as the whole. Fractals are useful in modeling structures (such as eroded coastlines or snowflakes), in which similar patterns recur at progressively smaller scales, and in describing partly random or chaotic phenomena such as crystal growth, fluid turbulence, and galaxy formation. If you study Gregg Braden's work, you will completely understand fractals."

"Boy, you never cease to amaze me!"

"Here, let me show you," he pulled up a *YouTube* video on fractals.

Awe-struck, I watched, "Wow, fractals are beautiful!"

Brandon exclaimed, "Wait until you see the movie!"

We were seated in the theater, and, all of a sudden, the lights went out and the dome filled with an intricate blue pattern. It felt as if we had been transported inside of the fractal. *I never knew math could be so beautiful,* I felt as if I had been shrunk, like in the movie *Inner Space* or *Honey, I Shrunk the Kids*. I felt my mind bending as we traveled in and out of the patterns within each fractal. Oh, how I have grown intellectually just hanging out with this kid.

When the movie got out, I took my phone out of my pocket to turn it back on. I had six missed calls from Anna. I called her immediately. When she answered, I asked, "Is something wrong?"

"No, I just couldn't get a hold of you, and it worried me."

"Anna, I took Brandon to see a movie about fractals. I should have let you know we would be late."

"Huh?"

"Precisely, I will let him tell you about it when we return."

The phone still had a lot of static, and I said, "Our connection is bad, we are on our way back, we'll see you soon." I hoped this clingy moodiness was a stage that would soon pass.

I looked over at Brandon, "I would give you advice about women, but I haven't figured them out myself yet!"

Brandon said, "It's okay, I am not dating yet, but when I do, I hope to find someone like my mom."

"Well, you will be a lucky man if you do."

Brandon replied, "I know. She is the best!"

They pulled into the parking area by the barn so Brandon could get the four-wheeler and check the horses before he went home. Anna started walking toward them. I waved at her, and when she came near, asked her, "How was your day?"

She whined, "I was lonely without you."

"Anna, why didn't you call Tori or go for a ride? What is up with you being so needy?"

That set her off again; she began sulking and would not answer him.

"Anna, please tell me what is wrong."

She walked away toward the house.

I hollered at her, "I will be up shortly."

I turned to Brandon.

"I wish I could figure out what goes on in a woman's mind, so I could avoid saying the wrong thing."

Brandon said, "Sometimes there are bigger issues than can be seen with the eyes, and it is Anna's journey, and only she can fix them."

"You are wise for such a young man, where did you get such wisdom?"

Brandon told him, "It is something that is passed down in my tribe. It is the way we are raised."

"I am certainly impressed."

We said, "Goodnight."

I told him, "I will see you in the morning."

I went up to the house with a sense of dread.

To my surprise, Anna seemed to have recovered from her previous mood. "I am sorry for earlier; I just had a boring day."

"All is forgiven." We went into the den where I read to her

to make up for his absence.

"Secrets try to enter our ears. Don't prevent them. Don't hide your face. Don't let us be without music and wine. Don't let us breathe once without being where you are."

I remarked, "I like this Rumi fellow; he has great ideas. I could use a little music and wine, how about you Anna?"

"That would be nice, at least the music. I must decline the wine."

"Another headache coming on, Anna?"

"I do feel one beginning."

I went to the wine cellar and selected a nice Pinot Noir. I loved the fragrant bouquet a Pinot offered. I took my glass back to the den and turned on a little romantic music. We lay there in silence just enjoying one another's company.

Finally, I broke the silence by asking her a question, "When we were in the daughter's bedroom the other day, did you notice the resemblance that the daughter has to you?"

Anna shrugged, "Maybe a little bit, but I did not really think we look that much alike."

"I thought you might be related."

"Anything is possible, but I don't think so."

Brandon wanted to talk to his mother when he got home. She was very tired from a long day in the hot sun at work but made sure to be attentive to her son's needs. They sat down at the small rustic table in the kitchen, her favorite place in the house, and she asked, "What is on your mind, Son?"

"Seth took me into Albuquerque today, and we had a wonderful day." He told her about the fractals and such. He finished with their visit to Silas and the concern he had after seeing something during that visit.

"What did you see that concerned you?"

"I saw Anna standing beside Silas; just like he said, she really is with him."

"We both are gifted with 'seeing,' and if Anna wants our help, we can help her crossover; you can assist me, and we can help her."

"Mom, you don't understand, it is not just Anna, Silas's daughter. It is Anna—the one engaged to Seth!"

Tori let out an audible gasp, "I knew there was something off about this situation and with Anna herself, but I never dreamed she was that Anna."

"Why do we see her as a person and not a ghost?"

"I believe it has more to do with our own brains and how they work than with Anna's manifestation."

She told Brandon she would do a bit of research before they

approached Anna and Seth. She warned him, "Until then, act as if nothing has changed. Even though she knows you know now, she may not realize that she has died, and it could be traumatizing to tell her. We will have to handle this situation with care. I may need to call in a more advanced and experienced medicine man to help us. Let's wait and see what I uncover in my research."

Tori headed into her room and booted up her laptop. She typed in a Google search and some interesting things appeared: one was an article about how people who have a brain injury can not only see spirits, but they also can feel them. That would explain why he could see her without being initiated into the world of the occult, and without believing in them . . . she would have to ask him about brain injuries he may have sustained during his football career.

She also happened upon a book titled *Setting Spirits Free* by Diana Palm. She was able to access the contents of the eBook, and it explained in detail how to help a soul crossover. Tori learned that once the spirits healed and moved into the light, they will be able to come back and be with their loved ones in a helpful way—a way in which they are not able to do as ghosts or trapped souls. The book explained the process on how to enter an altered state, a theta wave state, the same as what the shaman or medicine man uses to communicate with souls or spirits.

She began typing the steps to help Anna's crossover. She must start with breathing techniques, grounding herself and connecting to the light. This will create a connection from the earth plane to the spiritual plane, which makes it easier for the ghosts to find their way home. Tori thought that the technique was very much like many other healing techniques she learned from her grandmother.

The process goes like this: first, you must sit comfortably, connect with the breath, feel the energy from Mother Earth; second, move up through the bottoms of your feet and as it climbs, for it gently opens the chakras and then it rises to the crown and continues out and up to the universal energy or connective web and the creator; next, when the eyes begin to flutter, it is time to set an intention while connecting with the Creator or God; next, once you feel the connection is strong, you must make a command:

"Dear Creator, it is commanded to send any low-vibrating souls or ghosts that are currently in this home into your light now. Heal them with your unconditional love and transform them in your light in the highest way possible now. Thank you."

After this command, you drop your energy back into the home while picturing the home in your mind's eye or the third eye. Witnessing the energy or trapped soul move into the light, you may feel emotional during this part, but it will pass as the entire process takes only moments. You will sense when it is completed.

Tori thought that it would be easier than convincing Anna that she has died on the Earth plane. She would also like to incorporate her Native American customs such as lighting sage and cleansing herself and the house, and then using a prayer to the four directions before she began.

She needed to visit Silas and talk to him about letting his little girl go so that she can cross over into the light. If he does this, then Anna will be able to be with him whenever she wishes, and this will have a healing effect on him—instead of the energy drain he is now experiencing. But for now, she must rest, it was almost two in the morning. She would be very tired tomorrow!

Anna and I had had a relaxing evening last night, and once again I had a dreamless sleep. I guessed it was because I needed to rest. I went to the kitchen and saw Sadie busy at the stove.

I asked her, "What's for breakfast?"

"Oatmeal and cinnamon rolls."

I could barely contain my excitement; I loved cinnamon rolls, and I bet Brandon did, too. Sadie looked over her shoulder at me.

"Do you wish to hear the rest of the story about Silas?"

"Sure."

She said out loud, "Now where did I leave off? Oh, yes he was at the hospital; they had just pronounced Anna dead. Silas was beside himself, and he had to be sedated. The nurse called the ranch and had to have two ranch hands come and pick him up; one had to drive his car home, you see?

"They had sent him home with a prescription for tranquilizers, of which he became addicted. He said it was the only way he could get through his day. He took to the bottle not too long after that. He did not seem to care if he lived or died or if the ranch did for that matter.

"This was the second tragedy in his life. He lost his wife when Anna was around four years old, she liked to drink a bit and one night drank a bit too much and drown in the swimming pool. That was why he made sure Anna had swimming lessons, but it did not seem to matter; in the end, she drowned, too. Imagine losing both of your loves to drowning! No wonder the poor man lost it."

Anna came in just then; she must have heard the end of the conversation as she said, "Who were you talking about"?

I answered her, "Oh, no one, Sadie was just passing on a bit of local gossip."

Sadie said, "Humph!"

I was glad for the interruption as Sadie was beginning to rattle on, and none of it was too helpful for what I needed to know.

Brandon entered the kitchen and said, "EWWW WEEE, I could smell the cinnamon rolls at the barn!"

I winked at him, "Of course, you could!" And everyone

laughed.

Anna noticed Brandon was nervous and she asked him, "What is wrong?"

"Nothing really, I just have a lot on my mind today."

She let it go.

Brandon asked me, "Can I get off a bit early today? My mom doesn't have any afternoon tours today and wants me to go into Albuquerque with her."

"Sure, that would be fine. It will be nice for you and your mom to spend a bit of time together."

We got our chores done and set out to check the fences. The cattle were acting odd today; they were skittish and, as a matter of fact, so were the horses. Chase had snorted three times already, and he was as usually steady as they come. I checked the weather and could not find anything out of the ordinary.

What I couldn't know was Anna was nearby, she had changed form, but Ma'ii could still see her smoky essence. This definitely made the cattle and horses skittish; they had a perception that was higher than humans when it came to energy frequencies. Brandon could see that her agitation and anger were escalating, and it would continue to do so the longer she was trapped on this earth plane. He could not say anything though . . . he needed to wait for his mom and for their talk with Silas.

Anna called to him, she said, "I know you can still see me; I also know you know who I am."

He tried to ignore her, but she materialized directly in front of Cheveyo and made him rear. Brandon was a good rider and he stayed on, but I was alarmed. I told Brandon, "Head back to the barn and make sure your horse is okay; I can finish up here and will be there shortly."

Brandon did as he was told. Anna followed him, making the horse jumpy. He told her under his breath, "Please meet me in the barn." She disappeared. When he got to the barn, he untacked Cheveyo and got him in his stall, giving him a bit of hay to comfort him. He said, "What is going on Anna?"

"I want to know, are you going to tell Seth?"

He said, "No, or I would have already done so." He added, "Anyway, my mom has more experience with this, and she will come and speak with you."

"Oh."

"Anna, do you, uh, know you are . . ."

"Do I know what?" she demanded.

"Do you know you have died?"

She looked scared, "I had an idea, but wasn't sure; you just confirmed it. I did not know what was happening to me . . . I am becoming increasingly angrier lately."

"It is normal for trapped souls and . . ."

Just then I appeared, "Who are you talking to?"

Ma'ii said, "No, one, just Cheveyo."

"Do you always talk to your horse? And does he talk back?"

Ma'ii said, "Very funny!" Thankfully Anna had vanished, most likely returning to her material form in the house as she knew they would be up for lunch soon.

After lunch, I told Ma'ii, "You can go. I want to spend some time with Anna; I feel like I have been neglecting her lately."

"Thank you, Seth. Mom will be thrilled I am getting off earlier than she thought!"

I turned my attention to Anna, "Do you want to head up to the ridge? Maybe bring some cheese and wine; we could read poetry and watch the sunset."

"That would be lovely," She asked me. "Can you please get my book?"

"Sure thing, baby."

Sadie said, "I heard you mention wine and cheese, so I will pack the cheese and wine with a few other snacks for you."

"Sadie, you can take the rest of the day off if you'd like."

"Is that with pay?"

"Sure, why not? I am in a generous mood today," I turned to get the book from the den.

Sadie's voice stopped me, "Can I just ask you one thing, Seth?"

"Shoot."

"Who are you talking to all of the time?"

"Sadie, you are such a hoot!" I walked away laughing.

Sadie thought here we go again; another one was losing his mind in this house.

Before they headed to the ridge, I asked, "Anna, would you mind if I put a call into my brother?"

"No, I don't mind. I can wait." She overheard Seth telling his brother about my plan to buy the ranch and askin' for his help. He asked for his brother's email address and said he would email all of the info for the business plan in the morning. Then he said, "I love you," and hung up. Anna was eager to hear what his brother had said, "I could not help but overhear; is your brother willing to invest?"

"He said he will let me know after reviewing the paperwork and doing the business projections."

Anna smiled, "Well, at least, it wasn't a no."

I agreed. We took our supplies to the barn and packed up the horses and rode up to the ridge. I remembered to bring flashlights this time and had replaced the batteries with brand new ones. I loved being with Anna up there in the evening.

Tori got home shortly after Brandon, and they set off for Albuquerque. They signed in at the Sage Rehab Center and waited to be shown to Silas's room. Soon a nurse escorted them to his door. Silas was sitting near the window, and Anna was not there with him. This would give them the opportunity to speak to him without her first. They began by telling him about their gifts and that they knew he saw Anna because they could see her, too.

He said, "She is not here now."

Tori responded, "Yes, we know that. We would like to talk with you first, about Anna, and explain the process of assisting her into the light. This way she could cross over and come and go as she pleases to be with you. As it is now, she is trapped here and getting angrier every day. Once a person crosses over, he or she is of the light and can assist us on earth; he or she acts as a sort of an earth angel," Tori continued by telling Silas. "It would benefit you as well, and it may help you heal."

He agreed to help, "I will speak with Anna when she comes to see me."

Tori offered their assistance, but he declined, saying, "I can handle my little princess."

"Of course, you can."

She and Brandon wished him a good night and headed to the car. On the way home, Brandon told his mom about his encounter with Anna earlier that day.

"We are going to have to do an intervention soon. Anna's bad behavior will continue to escalate the longer she is here. Hopefully, she will speak with Silas soon."

Tori would have to talk with Seth and then with Anna and Seth. She could perform the crossing with the help of Brandon. It was just a matter of getting all of the parties involved on board.

After the sunset, Anna yawned, "I am tired and want to go back to the house."

I got out the flashlights and turned one on to give her, but it would not work. I thought how odd; I just bought new batteries! Oh well, at least the horses knew the way and are sure-footed as they travel this path almost daily. I tied George to his saddle horn, and we set off for the barn. Anna went to the house while I tended to the horses.

Anna showed up at Silas's side, "Hi Daddy, I missed you."

"We need to talk little girl."

She listened to what he had to say, but she vehemently disagreed with leaving him and me.

"It is for the best, my little princess."

She yelled, "NO!" and she was gone.

122

Silas was disheartened and wondered why he had listened to those strangers.

CHAPTER FIVE

Morning came again after a dreamless night. I sensed something was shiftin', and I could not quite put my finger on it. I needed to try and find investors today if I was goin' to get this ranch deal settled and behind me. I decided to ask my friend Dillon who might have money in the area and would be willin' to invest. Dillon was like a livin', breathin', Google data bank.

I made sure that Brandon was set to handle the day's work and headed over to Cerillos. I asked Dillon to meet me at the Black Bird Saloon; we had great sandwiches and cold beer. What better place to conduct a business meetin'? And it was the only place to eat in Cerrillos!

It happened to be attached to the building that housed the hotel that the character "Wren" lived in from the movie *Young Guns*;

the wall across the street was also in the movie. It was from my favorite scene: Billy Bonny is hiding behind the wall as Sherriff Brady is walking down the main street; Billy's hat floats out and lands at Brady's feet, shortly after Billy Bonny appears and says, "Reap the whirlwind, Sheriff Brady!" I loved that scene and *Young Guns I* and II are among my most treasured movies in my VHS collection! I still keep a mint condition VHS player to watch them on . . . someday I may move onto a DVD player . . . but I love nostalgia. I was excited to own a ranch where a lot of movie history was made.

I found a table on the patio and Dillon sauntered in just after I sat down.

"It is nice to see you, my friend. What is so urgent that you felt the need to call a business meeting?"

I laughed at that and answered him, "Well, I have asked Anna to marry me. If I am to be a good provider for her, I am goin' to need a means by which to provide. I looked into buying the ole' Ames place."

Dillon gave him a look.

"Now, now, I know what you are thinkin', but I have already added hay crops to bring in income as well as I have been running the spread almost single-handedly for over a year now. The problem is I have no investment capital. My brother, Sandoval, is very business oriented, and I have sent him all the paperwork for the ranch, spreadsheets, worth, income, taxes, etc., for the last three years, and he is working on the business plan as we speak. I also have asked him to think about investing; he would be my number cruncher, or accountant if ya' like."

Dillon nodded his head, "It sounds like you have a plan! The question is how do I figure into it?"

"I am glad you asked that. I was hopin' you would know who in this area would be interested in creating a ranch conglomerate and would have the funds to back up that interest."

Dillon tipped back in his chair and thought about it for a few minutes. He righted himself and told me, "Here is the thing, my last name is not Smith, it is Singleton, as in 'the son' of the wealthiest ranch owner in New Mexico, Henry Singleton. Although Daddy lives in Beverly Hills now, for some reason he prefers Cali to this splendid landscape. The family holdings are just over 1.2 million acres from Santa Fe to Roswell."

I was staring at him, dumbfounded. I could not even speak. I had to remind myself to take a breath and then questioned, "What? Why would you be working as a trail guide if you could be running one of those ranches?"

"Well, I, ya' see, I don't want to work that hard; I would rather do what I love and that is live free; work in rodeos, and meet interesting people every day, which I do as a cowboy and a trail guide."

I realized I didn't even know my friend, this man was a

stranger to me, or at least, he was now after this grand revelation. I said as much to Dillon, "I just realized I don't even know you!"

Dillon replied, "Seth, look, don't take it personally, if I went around broadcasting this fact, I would not know whom I can or cannot trust; when you have money, everyone wants to be your friend. But you, you know me, not the wealthy trust fund baby, but the real me. I would say we have a better relationship because of my keeping that to myself.

"The good news is, I do, in fact, have a trust fund and I could be an investor, or I could be 'THE' investor. On one condition—I am the silent partner, no one can know that the funding came from me; I do not want to blow my cover. I like my life here in Cerrillos. Or I can ask my father to buy the property; his specialty is buying up smaller parceled ranches. I would ask him to appoint you the ranch C.O.O."

I had to laugh at that, a ranch 'Chief Operations Officer,' a fancy title for the head ranch hand.

I confided, "I want to be able to buy into the financial ownership of the ranch, or have a trade, where my hours and the profits from the hay go towards my ownership. Like giving me a percentage every year we make a profit. It would be like profit sharing or similar to an employee-owned business, where I can buy into the company and my investment is met by the company— in this case the ranch."

"Seth, you don't give yourself enough credit; your brother is not the only one with business sense."

I continued, "I would prefer you to be the investor; do whatever makes you the most comfortable, either investing or talking with your father about buying the ranch. I will be grateful either way."

"Okay, Seth, I will have my lawyer work out the details; his name is Talbert Haskins," he—almost as an afterthought—added. "How much is owed on the ranch?'

"That is the best part; the note is only around five hundred thousand, and the ranch is worth about eight million in today's market. It is a perfect investment opportunity, if we sold it tomorrow, we would have an enormous return on our initial investment overnight. I would have to say that it is better than the stock market, wouldn't you?"

"And more stable," added Dillon.

"Talbert is also the lawyer for the ranch, so it will be easy for him to get it done. I will call him now."

We made plans to meet with the lawyer the following week. I hung up the phone saying, "Talbert can see us next Wednesday at two in the afternoon."

"That works for me; I will be sure to have the other guide scheduled for the afternoon rides that day."

I said, "See you then, my friend."

"You certainly will." We shook hands and headed in opposite directions.

When I returned to the ranch, I found Tori, Brandon, and Anna, sitting in the garden. I asked, "What's the occasion?"

Tori said, "I got off early as the last tour wasn't full, so the train didn't run; they will put the people on the next tour tomorrow at a discounted price for being delayed. I wanted to stop and see Brandon for lunch, and Anna invited us to eat in the garden."

"What a nice surprise."

Yet, I sensed a tension in the air and thought that it did not feel like a relaxed visit.

I asked Brandon, "Are you ready to get back to work?"

Brandon nodded, and they headed to the barn.

Tori waited until they were out of ear reach and turned to Anna; she continued with the pleas. She and Brandon had employed earlier before I walked up. "Anna, you must listen to reason; it is not fair to keep Seth tied to you when you are not truly bound to this earth. It is also not fair to you, to not enter into the light where you will be happy, filled with the most incredible love in the universe and able to come and go as you please helping your loved ones from the spiritual realm, instead of being trapped here in limbo."

Anna retorted, "But even you thought I was real! Seth KNOWS I am real!"

Tori explained the experiments that had been done with

people who have previous brain trauma. She told her of her suspicions that Seth had received trauma to his brain during his football days and that is why he felt her— why she appeared "real" to him.

"Anna, the mind is a powerful thing; it can convince us of anything we focus hard enough on. Brandon and I both knew something was amiss with you; you have drawn a lot of energy from your surroundings, people, and objects. Like the batteries, there are never batteries in the house that are not drained completely. Brandon noticed that you and Sadie never interact; he mentioned it to me, and I told him I sensed something was not right with you as well.

"If you allow us to help you, we can perform a ceremony where you will be able to cross over. Once it is done, you will be released from your prison between earth and the spiritual realm, you will see the illusion of physical love fade away to be replaced by true love from the Divine."

Anna glared, "I bet you want him for yourself, and that is why you are doing this!"

Tori shot back, "Whether I am interested in him or not is irrelevant Anna; I want to help you. If you stay, your soul will become more and more tormented . . ."

"GET OUT!" Anna spat the words at her. "I know you will tell Seth so you can take him from me!"

Tori got up and, as she was walking away, turned back to Anna and replied in a soft tone, "I shall not do that because I care about him, and I care about you; we must come to a mutual decision to tell him. It will be the best way to reduce the effect of the news and the harm it will induce," Tori added. "Please think about it. Anna, I am on your side."

Brandon and I were tinkering around in the equipment barn, and I ran the idea of his staying on and becoming a part of the ranch crew once I purchased it. "Brandon, I would love to have you stay on here and maybe one day become a partner."

"I would love to, but I have to attend school, so it would only be in the summer that I could be here.

"I will accommodate you any way I can. I love working with you. I believe I have learned as much from you as I have tried to teach you. You will be an asset to this ranch."

"Thank you for being so kind. Seth, I have a question for you: do you believe in spirits?"

I looked perplexed at the change of subject but replied to him, "I have never thought about it one way or another." I added, "Why do you ask?"

"I don't know. I have been thinking about spirits lately. I sometimes think I hear them when I am alone in the ruins. The voices of the past haunting the present."

I saw through his charade, "Are you still on that kick about Anna being the ghost that you saw with her father?" I didn't wait for Brandon to respond, "Well, I guess anything is possible. Now can you hand me that wrench; we want to make sure this bailing equipment stays in tip-top shape over the winter."

Brandon thought that it was going to take a lot to convince me of Anna being a ghost. When Brandon got home, he asked his mom, "How did the rest of the visit with Anna go?"

Tori answered, "I am afraid it did not go very well at all; she is vehement that she is staying on the earth, and she became quite violent. She seems to view me as her enemy now, and she fears I am trying to take Seth away from her."

Brandon whispered, "That may be very close to the truth."

Tori looked sad and told her son, "Even if I wish it, I would not try to come between him and Anna. At least not now. When she crosses over, she will see that true love wants the best for others, and there is no jealousy in Heaven. There are many other things that would have to happen before I can be involved with Seth." *Like he must want me also*, she thought, but did not voice it aloud.

"I know, Mom, I would love to have him in my life too; I wish he was my father."

To which his mother replied, "If wishes were gold, we would be wealthy beyond our dreams. Now head on up to bed, Son. I think I will meditate a bit before I turn in."

Tori burned some sage and lit her white candles; she sat in her relaxed pose, ankles crossed, hands rested on her knees, palms up. Palms up was for receiving. She asked the great spirit to guide her in doing what was best for all involved and to show her the way, which path would bring success. She began to gently rock to and fro; her eyes began to flutter, and she entered that place just outside of her material self.

She met her guides there. She was told that she would not have to do this alone; her guides and the angels were working behind the scenes to assist her. They have even asked Anna's mother to appear to her and ask Anna to join her in the light.

Tori slowly came out of her theta state as it took a few moments to go from 4 to 7 cycles per second in the brain to a brainwave frequency of 14 to 28 cycles per second. It took many years to master going so deeply into a meditative state, but it was the best way for her to receive Divine guidance from the creator.

After her meditation, she began studying the techniques to cross Anna over; she would like to know if Silas had any luck talking with his daughter.

Tori had a feeling that his health was suffering because he was one of the energy sources for Anna. She was also drawing energy from Seth and anyone else that was around her; that is why she appears so real to those that can see. I often complained of being tired. She would bet Sadie felt tired, too. She would have to ask Brandon if he felt drained when he was around Anna. Tori learned long ago how to protect from energy vampires and such. She grounds herself to Mother Earth and wraps herself in divine light daily. It was time for rest now; she was ready for bed.

Anna and I were relaxing on the couch, and she asked me to read to her from her new book again. "I would be much obliged to read to you, my love."

I took it from the side table.

"*Burning with longing-fire, wanting to sleep with my head on your doorsill, my living is composed only of this trying to be in your presence.*"

"I feel that way about you, Seth. Read another poem, please."

I continued:

"*I love this giving my life to you, or to anyone who knows* someone who knows you, caught as I am in your curling hair, inside your Kashmiri-witch eyes."

I looked at Anna. "Well, what do ya' know? He wrote one about me and how I feel about you, too!"

Anna giggled, "Just one more . . ."

How he could deny her when it brought her such pleasure.

"I planted roses, but without you they were thorns. I hatched peacock eggs, snakes were inside. I played the harp, sour music. I went to the eighth heaven, it was the lowest hell."

I thought that was a dark note to end on so added one more:

"If I gave up sanity, I could fill a hundred versions of you. There is no liquid like a tear from a lover's eye."

"Oh, Seth, I love the timber of your voice when you read to me; it makes me feel safe and loved. Your voice is like angel wings wrapped around me."

I thought that was the sweetest thing anyone had ever said about him, and I told her so. I asked Anna if I could talk to her a moment before we headed up to bed. "I had a conversation with Dillon today about finding investors for the ranch."

"Does Dillon know any?"

"Better than that, HE is going to invest. Apparently, he has money, but he doesn't want anyone to know. He is willing to be a silent partner."

She squealed delightedly, "That means we can live here forever!"

He kissed her before saying, "Yes, Darlin', it sure does."

It was time for bed; it seemed I never got enough sleep, so we headed up the stairs, but Anna wanted to race. I took the stairs two at a time and beat her by a nose! We fell on the bed laughing. Anna looked at me, "I never want to leave you, not even when we're ghosts; you are the one I shall always love the most . . ." I just looked at her and then kissed her passionately.

That night I had a wonderful dream. I was hovering over Anna, and as I gazed into her eyes, I felt adrift in a sea of blue. She fascinated me by how she could stir my need for her to a fever pitch within seconds. I bent down and brushed her lips with mine, and then I traced the flow of her collarbone with soft kisses as I slipped her shirt from her shoulder, exposing her breast. It was a perfect mound, topped by an erect nipple. I teased her with little licks and nibbles. As she arched her back, she moaned, lower baby, lower. I unbuttoned her shirt, exposing both breasts, and kissed them before moving down to her tummy. I slowly unzipped her jeans with one hand; I slid them from her hips, dipping low while flicking his tongue on her mound. She tasted sweet. She arched and bucked beneath my mouth until I had to enter her. I held nothing back, rolling them over so that Anna was on top. She rode him expertly, almost to the verge of orgasm, but I held back, withdrawing from her and flipping her over. I did not wait long to fill her void. She moaned and wiggled as I pulsed within her and she began to grind on him. I bent low and bit her on the back like a stallion; our passion flared like the hottest flame. I yearned to possess her, claim her as his. I was burning so hot with desire I thought it may consume him, consume us. I sucked her neck as I pushed hard into her and flooded her with my seed. Anna's moans turned into screams as she clutched the sides of the bed, and then faded to whimpers.

She gave no reprieve as she began to move again; she tightened her thighs, squeezing harder and harder, provoking me to cum again. I fell to the bed gasping for air. She rolled into me, holding me close and kissing me ever so lightly on my ribs as her hand played with my chest hair.

I opened my eyes and rolled over to gaze at the clock; it was 6 AM, and I had to head to the barn. Ma'ii would arrive at seven. I felt as if sleep had eluded me. I flung the covers off and kissed Anna on the forehead, and then headed to the bathroom.

I looked in the mirror and the dream came flooding back in vivid detail, it was as if she had wanted to make sure I never left her; she was branding me as hers, the thought of the dream made me tingle, and I was overcome with a need to have her to go to the bed and take her once more. But work awaits, and the boy would be here soon - time for coffee as I felt drained.

I entered the kitchen where Sadie was making eggs over okra with biscuits and hash browns, it smelled delicious, I told her she better be sure there was enough for a growing boy and a hungry man, she laughed and said, "Isn't there always enough?"

Ma'ii came in as if on cue and announced, "I am starving!" Then he proceeded to heap his plate full. Sadie and I had to laugh at our inside joke. Ma'ii asked, "Where is Anna?"

Sadie gave us a sideways glance. *What is up with that woman? Always looking at me like I have horns or something.* I addressed Brandon, "She is still in bed, wrapped up like a babe in her blankets."

He remarked, "Must be nice!"

We went to the barn and started our daily routine; he reminded me that this Saturday was his birthday party. "I know it is, and we are all looking forward to it." I thought to myself I will have to remind Tori, Sadie, and Anna to get everything ready.

CHAPTER SIX

The day was uneventful, and we got done early. I told Brandon, "You can go home if you want to."

He said, "I like hangin' out with you."

"Why don't we take the horses over to Cerrillos and take a ride in Cerrillos Hills Park?" I was eager to go. "While we are there," I added, "we can see if Dillon is up for joining us."

"That would be cool; maybe he would like to come to my party. Let's invite him."

"You could ask him; I bet he would love to come. Let's get the rig ready."

We loaded up the horses and tack and set off for Cerrillos.

We pulled into the Broken Saddle Stables, and I went in search of Dillon. I found him filling water troughs.

"Hey, mi amigo bueno, I have a bit of free time and wanted to spend some QT with the boy; Brandon would like to meet you, and we both would like to know if you would join us on a ride in the park. You could give the boy a tour."

Dillon smiled, "I would love to take you guys on a tour of the hills; I just have to check with the other guide and make sure he can handle the business for a few hours."

He came back a few moments later, "Jimmy would be happy to take over for a while; I will head up the hill to get my horse, Pearl."

Brandon and I tacked up our mounts while he was getting Pearl. When Dillon rode up, I made the introductions. When I said, "Dillon, I would like you to meet Brandon . . ."

Brandon piped in, "I prefer to be called Ma'ii."

Dillon winked, "Then Ma'ii it is!"

We set off for the park entrance at a trot. On our way to the trail, we passed an old cemetery, and Ma'ii commented that he had family buried there.

"Oh," said Dillon and I in Unison.

Ma'ii told of his grandmother's passing. He professed, "I believe the spirit and soul leave the body because they are energy contained in matter when we are alive, but when we pass, the body is discarded, and the 'person' is no longer there. So, I feel no need to visit cemeteries for the sake of communing with relatives as they are now free from their bodies and can be anywhere and everywhere."

"Interesting concept," noted Dillon.

I affirmed, "Yeah, he is full of interesting concepts, and is very wise for such a young man."

Dillon had to agree.

We were almost to the entrance when there was a ruckus above our heads. Dillon pointed out a raven's nest on the ridge.

"That breeding pair is holding their territory and will discourage other birds and other ravens from intruding upon it. Both parents take care of the nest. They are very intelligent birds and quite a bit noisy."

Ma'ii commented, "I love ravens; they have a mystical significance." Dillon wanted to know more about ravens, so Ma'ii continued his narrative, "They are generally a symbol of death and the underworlds, yet, this is not always a literal death; it means that something, positive or negative, is transforming in your life and it may be dramatic. The raven spirit can guide you through this transformation. They consume other creatures' remains, and this lends to them the symbol of cleansing, possibly something old, or unhealthy needs to be purged from your life.

"They are also magicians and compel one to study that realm, the one where magic dwells. They are masters of time and a time lesson may be in your future; they mainly are the symbol of rebirth. They remind you to boost powers of observation and bring things into the light as well as improve communication skills. When a raven has entered your life, you will not want for mystical adventures or spiritual surprises."

Dillon was agape.

I told him, "Close your mouth Dillon, or you are gonna' eat a fly!"

Dillon snapped to and asked no one specifically, "Where did this kid come from?"

I answered, "Farmington," and they all laughed.

Ma'ii explained, "My mother is Navajo, and she and I are both gifted 'seers'; we come from a long line of medicine people."

Dillon teased, "I can 'SEE' that!"

Ma'ii laughed but added, "It is a serious matter."

We came up to the entrance of the turquoise mine, and it was Dillon's turn to shine with his knowledge of the mining history. He began, "The Cerrillos Hills are the most mineral rich area in New Mexico; all of the main minerals are present for mining, yet, not in one place so large-scale mining is not supported. There are also Silver, Gold, Manganese, Galena, Copper, and Iron mines in the park, but they are plugged ten feet down with dirt or foam, so people do not enter them and become trapped. The turquoise mines are claimed, and the owners can press trespass charges if you enter the mines. The Park has been granted pass-through access only. Turquoise pieces and jewelry can be purchased at the mining museum in town."

Ma'ii piped in, "The first miners in this district were Puebloans; they came from the thriving communities in the Galisteo Basin, and, at that time, the area was called Sierra de San Mateo."

Dillon teased, "Maybe you would like my job?"

"Maybe! On a serious note, though, I study ancient peoples and love archeology and anthropology."

Dillon nodded, "It shows."

After they rode up to the view where you could see three states, one being Colorado and another Arizona, they looped back to the stables.

Ma'ii asked Dillon, "Would you like to come to my party on Saturday evening?"

Dillon accepted, "I would love to come sit a spell with you, I love parties."

On the ride back home in the truck, Ma'ii told me, "The symbol of the Raven is very prophetic for you in this moment; you should meditate on that . . . maybe."

"Sure, I will consider doing that." Of course, I changed the subject and began talking about rodeos.

Brandon hoped that I would come around and see the 'light' so to speak, because if Anna agreed, they would soon be crossing her over. If I did not face the reality of this situation, I would be emotionally traumatized. When a person was a non-believer, it was not an easy task to break the chains on his/her mind, so he/she could see there is more to life than what meets the eye. There is a spiritual world wrapped into the material world. Becoming aware is all that is needed to lift the veil. Ma'ii felt that I knew in my heart that this was true. I just needed to accept it, and maybe his mom could be more persuasive in helping me to understand.

It was Friday, and Tori had a lot to do in preparation for Brandon's party tomorrow. Saturdays were always busy days for tours; she had asked for the day off so she could be at her son's birthday party. She had great bosses! They asked Lilia to cover for her this Saturday. She owed Lilia big. Now she would pitch in and help the others all day, instead of relying on them to get it done. She needed to get over there and take the supplies she had gathered to them, but first she wanted to pop in on her friend Leonie. She was a wise woman and always was able to give sound advice.

She drove the short distance to Leonie's Bed and Breakfast. Tori hollered, "Yoo-hoo! Leonie, are you home?"

Leonie answered, "Yes, I am in the treatment room doing yoga."

"Oh, I am sorry. I did not mean to interrupt you."

Leonie assured her, "It is fine" and asked her to join her in a few poses as they talked.

Tori rolled out a mat she had taken from the basket in the corner and joined her friend in pigeon pose. She stretched one of her legs behind her and then brought her knee and ankle to her wrists. She then laid her other leg down on the mat parallel to the top edge, and then stretched up first before leaning over her leg. She loved that hip opener! Once they were in position, Tori told Leonie about her predicament, and how Seth would not accept the facts. "He is not a believer in the spiritual realm."

Leonie advised her, "Your approach may be too direct; most people are afraid of what they do not know. Possibly you could find some proof and approach him subtly with it, thus, imparting your wisdom by showing evidence that backs up what you are telling him."

"You are such a wise Sage; I knew you could help me see this from a better perspective. As an added bonus, I now have open hips."

"Please stay and join me for the savasana meditation, and then I will make you my famous flower tea."

They took the corpse pose position on their backs.

Leonie whispered, "Palms up for receiving, palms down for listening, or the yoga chin mudra for giving."

Tori kept her hands in the position to receive as she would

take all the guidance she could get.

After they closed the session, Leonie made her famous flower tea. It was such a soothing tincture; Tori called it tonic for the soul. Leonie grew all of the herbs in her greenhouse and dried them herself; she had all sorts of lotions, potions, and teas on her shelves.

As Leonie boiled water and steeped the tea, a chicken walked up to her and circled her legs.

Tori asked her, "Have you moved the girls from their coop into the kitchen?"

She laughed at the absurdity of that statement, "Heavens no, Greta is hurt and needed a little TLC, so I brought her in. Her sisters were ganging up on her and hurting her."

"The chicken as a spiritual animal means enlightenment and illumination." Leonie clarified, "When a chicken enters your life, it is about the power of your voice and heeding your inner voice. It shows you that you need to speak up about something that has been bothering you for a while or you will carry this burden around forever."

Tori could not help but smile at the synchronicity of having the chicken in the kitchen and its profound significance to her situation—the very situation she had just asked Leonie for guidance with and meditated on. Well, she now had her answer loud and clear. The chicken seemed to know she needed confirmation! She thanked her friend for the tea and told her, "I am having a party for

Brandon's birthday tomorrow, and you are welcome to stop by; it is at the old Ames' place. He would love to see you!"

Leonie said, "I might pop in for a few." She hugged her friend goodbye. On the left side, she always said. Heart to heart. Tori had a great affection for Leonie and her uniqueness.

Tori pulled onto the lane heading to the ranch, and she noticed a horse trailer pulling in behind her. She wondered who would be bringing horses here. Lost in thought, she parked at the house. As she opened her car door, she heard a familiar voice say, "Hey, Mom, what are you doing here?"

She said, "Oh, Brandon you startled me; I came to set up for your party."

He said, "Cool."

"Where have you two been?"

Brandon told her all about the ride and meeting Dillon. "He said he was coming to the party and he is single . . ."

"Stop trying to play matchmaker, and you reminded me that I also asked Leonie to come."

Brandon smiled, "I love Leonie, and it will be great for her to come."

Tori waved at me and went in to find Sadie and Anna. She saw Sadie in the kitchen squeezing lemons. Tori said, "Hello, what can I do to help set up for the party? I see you already have the lemonade started."

Sadie told her, "You can check on the carrot cake; it is cooling over there; it will need to be frosted and decorated."

"I can frost it, but I should leave the decorating part to the professional."

Tori heard a noise and turned to see Anna enter the room, she said, "Hello," and asked Anna if she wanted to join them in the decorating.

Anna said, "Planning and placement are my specialties, and I can help with that."

The women worked diligently for hours, only breaking for dinner. The men joined them at the table, and Tori hoped she would have time to speak with me alone later; it was always hard to speak freely here as Anna did not like us being alone and was bound to overhear. She, knowing Anna would never venture out, had a plan; she would invite them to hear music at the Mineshaft tonight.

Once everything for the party was in place, Tori said, "Thank you, everyone, especially you Sadie for staying late tonight on a Friday."

Sadie said, "At my age, Friday is just another day."

Tori then extended the invitation to Anna and me, "How would you two like to come and hear music at the Mineshaft tonight?"

Anna bowed out just as expected but I exclaimed, "That sounds like a great time!"

I looked at Anna, "Would you mind me going out for a bit?"

She replied, "Not at all." However, her eyes said something else.

Brandon suggested, "I can stay here with you, Anna; we can plan the music for tomorrow, and I can even stay all night if you want as I have to come here early in the morning anyway."

"Sure, Brandon, I like talking with you; you are very informative and informed, and I always learn something new!"

"I have to go home and get ready," then Tori added. "Should I meet you there?"

I decided to ride in with Tori. "If you can wait a minute, I would like to ride in with you." I told her, "I thought Brandon wanted to spend the night; there are plenty of guest rooms, so you could stay too. Why don't we swing by your place and pick up what you need before the show?"

Tori agreed and headed out to her Jeep to wait, as she needed to load the leftover supplies into her Jeep anyway.

I went upstairs to get ready. Anna and Brandon went into the den to plan tomorrow's entertainment.

When I came down to say goodbye to her, I overheard Brandon asking if they could have a bonfire . . .

I said, "I hate to interrupt, but I am leaving now, and I need to hug my girl."

Anna stood up and stiffly hugged me. I knew there was a

storm brewing beneath that pretty face. I would deal with that later; right now, I was headed to Madrid to have a bit of fun.

On the way in Tori tried small talk but decided that she needed to address the elephant in the room, and the sooner, the better. She began, "Seth, I am glad you want to stop by my house as I have something I want to show you. We also need to have a serious talk about Anna, you, and the situation you are in."

I got quiet, and my facial features looked as if they were set in stone. I took about five minutes and then said, "Please not this again, not tonight."

Tori retorted, "Seth, you have to face the facts. I have spoken with Silas and Anna. YOUR Anna is also his daughter, who has passed away. She never crossed into the light and is trapped here; I can help her cross over into the light. She can then come and go on the earth plane as she pleases. Once a soul crosses over, they become a spirit and can assist us here on the earth plane. As it stands now, she is trapped and will become angrier every day, acting out until harm may come . . ."

I yelled, "I NEED PROOF!"

Tori remained calm, "I knew you would; that is why I wanted you to come into my home and look at my photo album from when Anna and I were in our late teens and early twenties, just before Anna had her accident."

I was still stewing about this topic but offered to take a look at her photos.

Tori pulled onto Back Road, taking a left onto Grasshopper Road which curved into Waldo Mesa. After about a quarter of a mile, she stopped in front of her little bungalow. It was a cute house; like her car, it suited her. They went inside and she took the albums off the shelf in the den.

They sat on her funky sofa, and she opened the first book; I could not believe my eyes! There stood Anna, her blue eyes intensely staring back at me, next to Tori. I asked no one in particular, "How can this be?"

Tori said, "I know this is hard to comprehend, Seth, but it is true. Brandon and I have both seen her with her father and because we can 'see' she appears to us. Have you ever noticed that no one else can see her? That she avoids coming around company and guests? Sadie never interacts with her; you never see her eat. She seems real to you because a human brain can manufacture a reality which feels real. I have this article from the magazine *Popular Mechanics* explaining how you 'feel' her.

"She is also powerful because she draws energy from her father, you, and other energy sources at the ranch. Do you ever notice you feel drained and tired most of the time when you are around her? Brandon and I can see spirits or ghosts, yet, she seemed real to us. Because her energy field is strong, she appears as real, not an apparition."

I could not take my eyes off the photo; I had a tear rolling down one cheek. I finally tore my gaze away to look at Tori.

"This is so unreal; how can this be happening? I know I love her; she is real!" His voice became a whisper. "At least, to me, she is."

Tori sympathized with him. She explained, "We will have to confront her and get her to agree to the ceremony so I can help her to cross over. It would be best to wait until after the birthday party."

"Yes, I need time to digest this and decide the best way to handle it."

"Of course," she replied, "Let's just go and have fun tonight, and we can deal with this on another day. It may help if you talk with her father again."

CHAPTER SEVEN

Tori grabbed what she needed, and we headed to the Mine Shaft. As we entered through the shaft for which the place got its name, we saw Dillon already seated at a table on the patio near the band. We asked to join him. A few moments later Leonie walked in, and we waved to her to join us. She came over and introductions were made.

Dillon and Leonie spoke simultaneously, "I have seen you around . . ."

Everyone laughed at that.

The band began with a Rock-a-Billy song, and the first round of beer was delivered. The group was having a great time; Leonie and Dillon even danced a bit. Tori noticed that I was drinking heavily. It was not her place to stop me, but she was going to have to deal with me on the way home.

After the last session ended, Tori suggested we head back to the ranch. I was now slurring my words and walking a bit unsteady. She employed Dillon to help her. Together they got me into her Jeep. Tori gave Leonie and Dillon hugged goodbye; she hopped into the driver's seat.

Dillon said, "I will follow you home and help you get him into the house."

She thanked him, and then told Leonie, "I will see you tomorrow beautiful." We drove off. Dillon was right behind her. She contemplated how she would handle this situation with Anna; there were sure to be fireworks when they arrived with my drunk ass in tow. She turned into the drive and shored up her reserve before arriving at the house.

She parked her car, and Dillon joined her on the passenger side to extract a now me snoring; I apparently reeked of alcohol! They wrestled me out and each took an arm over a shoulder, and they began the arduous task of getting me inside. They got as far as the mudroom before Anna came at them full force. She was ranting about how "we" allowed Seth to get drunk then began flinging accusations at us. *Well at me*, thought Tori as Dillon was oblivious to her.

At least Tori was ready for this. Tori explained, "He is a grown man and 'we' had nothing to do with the state he is in; he made his own decisions." She added, "We share your concerns about how much alcohol he has consumed."

Anna preceded them to "their" room upstairs. Dillon offered to get me undressed and tucked in; the girls went out into the hallway. He wondered if Tori drank a bit too much as well. She was mumbling to herself the entire way up the stairs. He thought he could still hear her in the hallway.

Anna immediately asked Tori, "What have you done to make Seth drink?"

Tori assured her, "I have done nothing." She suggested that maybe Seth just overindulged as he has been under stress to buy the ranch and get the wedding underway."

Anna retorted, "Oh, now it is my fault?"

"Anna, please calm down; it is no one's fault, and you should be glad that he wants to provide for your future."

Anna took a moment to compose herself and said, "I guess you're right. Thank you for getting him home."

"It's okay; I am glad to help," she was tired and told Anna. "I need to rest." Then she headed to her guest room, looking over her shoulder she said, "Goodnight, see you in the morning, Anna, it is party day tomorrow."

As she headed back into her room, Anna murmured, "Yes, it is." She could not believe the state that I was in. Regrettably, I had done this once before, and she wondered if I had issues with substance use. After all, she has had past experience; it was the reason her mother drowned. One too many martini's poolside.

She thanked Dillon for helping get me in bed; he just turned and walked away. Anna thought how odd he was.

Dillon knocked on Tori's bedroom door before he left; he wanted to ask her something. Tori answered the door in a flimsy nightgown, so Dillon became distracted for a moment. Then, he regained his composure and asked her, "Why were you arguing with yourself while we brought Seth in?"

Tori explained, "It is a long story, and I would be glad to meet you next week for lunch to discuss it," she added. "I am way too tired to deal with it right now. I will see you tomorrow at the party." She kissed him on the cheek and bid him a "Good night."

He said, "I will lock up on my way out, and I look forward to the party. Good night."

That night I slept like the dead. I did not dream, and I awoke with a pounding in my head that mimicked a jackhammer.

With a sour look on her face, Anna said, "Glad to see you are still with us; hope you feel absolutely miserable."

I responded with a grunt, "Why do you have to be so

mean?"

"I am not just mad at you for your lack of discretion where drinking is concerned, but I also feel that you may have a problem with alcohol; as in, you are an alcoholic!"

In complete disbelief, I turned, "Anna, you are worried about my drinking? On what basis?"

She said meekly, "This is the second time you came home from the Mine Shaft drunk in the last couple of months."

"I drank two times, and now you think I am a drunk, huh?"

Telling me about her mother, she stressed, "I cannot bear to see another person I love die because of an addiction."

I took her in my arms and as I held her close, I assured her, "Hun, don't worry about me that way, I was just lettin' off some steam with friends. I am under a lot of stress trying to buy the ranch and provide a future for us; all you need to do is worry about the wedding."

Anna smiled at that and told him to take some aspirin as it was going to be a long day." After all, we have a party to get ready for!" She trounced from the room and headed to the kitchen.

Brandon, Tori, and Sadie were in the kitchen when Anna entered. Tori inquired, "How is Seth?"

Anna answered, "Like death warmed over!"

Tori giggled, "It deserves him right."

Sadie looked over her shoulder to see why Tori was speaking

to Seth in the third person but saw he was not there. She thought to herself, *Crazy must be catching like a virus around here.* She asked, "Miss Tori, would you like some more herbal tea?"

"I would love another cup," She took her cup to Sadie.

I dragged myself into the kitchen and I really did look like death warmed over! I grumbled, "Coffee!!!!!"

Sadie cried, "Lordy, looks like someone tied one on last night!" She thrust a cup at him and pointed to the coffee.

Anna and Tori laughed at her lack of sympathy. Tori commented, "It deserved him right for his poor behavior and lack of judgment."

I complained, "Y'all are ganging up on me this morning!"

Brandon piped in, "I for one am glad to see you, Seth, and I cannot wait to get started on the party preparations."

I told him, "As soon as I eat and get my fuel down, I will be raring to go, and, by the way, HAPPY BIRTHDAY Brandon!"

Dillon knocked on the door before waltzing into the kitchen; everyone noticed that Sadie, handing him a steaming cup of coffee and a kiss on the cheek, was much more obliging to him.

I mumbled, "I see who counts around here."

Everyone laughed but me; I just sat sipping my "fuel" with a scowl on my face.

Tori commented, "I hope your mood improves before the party starts and the guests arrive."

Brandon's mouth widened, "All of the guests are already here."

Tori said, "Well, except Leonie. She agreed to come."

"Oh right, Mom, I forgot."

After breakfast, we guys headed to the barn to let the horses out to graze, as there would be no fence work today. Brandon asked, "Can we take a hayride later in the evening as part of the festivities?"

I said, "Only if you quit using such fancy words."

"Okie Dokie, is that better? I will hook up the tractor to the trailer and fill it with straw."

I began to feel better and a smile crept on my face. I sure loved seeing the boy happy.

Dillon arrived, "How can I help?"

I answered, "Well, we have to move the furniture up to the patio where the girls are decorating. Put some straw bales around the fire pit and get the wood ready."

"Okay, I am on it."

I instructed Brandon, "Wait to load the straw so we can haul the furniture up to the house with the wagon." We began loading everything into the wagon.

Brandon overheard me ask Dillon if he had looked into the business deal yet. Dillon replied he had, and his broker was working on freeing up the money, so we should meet with the lawyer next week sometime. I thanked him and said I would make the appointment with Talbert.

When we reached the patio, it was transformed into a place to hold a proper shindig. There were twinkle lights and table clothes with assorted decorations highlighting his interest in archeology, fractals, and even a few rodeo-themed pieces as well; like professionals, the girls had made it flow together. We guys set the furniture up where we were instructed to do so and then left the ladies to clean it. We proceeded to the fire pit.

When we were done, Dillon complimented, "It sure looks like a party is happening here!" We guys agreed and took the tractor back down so we could fill the wagon with straw for the hayride.

Once we got to the barn, Dillon said to me, "I need to ask you something about Tori."

I said, "Shoot."

"Well, err," Dillon replied, "I don't know how to say this, except to just come on out and say it; Tori was having a conversation with someone who was not there when we were carrying you into the house last night. I asked her about it, but she put me off, said she would explain later."

I asked, "Did she mention the name Anna?"

Dillon scratched his head, "Yeah, I think that was the name she used."

I asked, "Are you sure you did not see anyone else there?"

Dillon looked me straight in the eye, "Seth, there was NO

ONE ELSE THERE!"

"No need to get all worked up; I just wondered if maybe you didn't see the other person."

"I already told you; there was no one else to see." He questioned, "Is she okay? I mean she doesn't have mental issues, does she?"

"No, there are some strange things goin' on here at the ranch, and I will also have to talk about it later. Sorry, Dillon."

Dillon asked, "Will this strange activity affect my investment?"

I assured him, "No, nothin' like that. No worries, it is just personal stuff." As an afterthought, I asked Dillon, "Do you believe in ghosts?"

"Sure, I reckon they exist."

"Hmmm, I am on the fence about that subject, but I am beginning to think it could be so."

We worked in silence for a few minutes, and Dillon asked, "Is this situation pertaining to a ghost?"

"It could be. We can talk about it after the party."

Dillon agreed. Brandon had overheard most of the conversation and was glad that I was starting to believe the fact that Anna was definitely a ghost. He would have to let his mom know, but for now, they had a party to tend to.

Everyone went into the house to clean up and when they

entered the kitchen there was a mixture of aromas floating in the air. The mouthwatering smells made everyone rush to get ready; there was nothing better than Sadie's cooking and tonight was going to be a feast!

Sadie was just putting the finishing touches on the cake. She had already set the table, and I was getting the grill lit so the steaks could be custom cooked when Leonie walked onto the patio area. She exclaimed, "Wow! This is amazing!" She turned to Brandon and, as she handed him a package, said, "Happy Birthday!"

He thanked her with a hug. They walked over and sat down by Tori and Dillon. Anna was absent as she said she had another one of her headaches and needed to lie down. Tori thought that this was a good thing as it would be tough to explain to Dillon and Leonie who they were responding to. *Leonie has the gift, so maybe it would just be hard for Dillon to understand.* She had a feeling he already suspected something—although it was probably more along the lines of her being crazy.

I was taking orders for the rib eyes.

Brandon said, "Well done please."

"That is gonna' ruin the flavor!"

"I cannot eat undercooked meat."

I laughed, "Since it is your birthday, well done it is."

Dillon said, "I will take mine mooing; just smack it on the ass as it walks by."

I responded, "I will make it rare then."

I looked over at Tori and Leonie arching an eyebrow, "Ladies? What'll it be?"

They both spoke simultaneously, "Medium well." Everyone laughed.

"Sadie, are you staying?"

She frowned, "As much as I would love to, I need to get home and tend to Vernon, but thank you for the invite." She headed for her car and drove off.

Tori took over as hostess, setting the table and getting drinks. I looked over at Tori and the thought of her in the kitchen serving me breakfast flashed through his mind. I felt guilty immediately and then conflicted as I realized I was most likely engaged to a ghost, not another woman. I let those thoughts go so I could continue to enjoy the party. Tonight, I was drinking lemonade— and not the hard kind— as I was still recovering from yesterday's escapades.

Everyone was eating and drinking to their hearts' content. Finally, it was time to serve the cake and open the gifts. The cake was delicious; Dillon and Brandon each had two slices, and the girls' shared one slice. I handed Brandon a hand carved wooden box. Brandon opened it and found inside an I.O.U. for two VIP passes to the rodeo. At the bottom was a note that the passes will be waiting at will-call for them the day of the rodeo. He said, "WOW! I, thanks,

I love the rodeo."

I told him, "Dillon played a hand in setting it up, and he arranged it so we can be back behind the chutes with the Cowboys."

Brandon thanked Dillon as well and he hugged me. Emotion stirred in my chest as Brandon hugged me, and I realized I was starting to care a whole lot about this boy.

Next, he opened the gift from Leonie. She had made a healing pouch for him. It was the most beautiful pouch he had ever seen; the stitching was intricate with peyote and energy lines as the border around a cross with hearts at the ends, signifying the four directions. She had stitched quills onto the bag to make the patterns. It was made of leather and held together with sinew, just as the Navajo made them. Leonie had added horsehair tassels.

She confided to the group, "The tassels are in fact, from Brandon's horse, Cheveyo." She turned to Brandon, "Your mom had brought some of his hair to me so I could make it special for you."

Two feathers decorated with beaded wraps were fastened to the strap that went around his neck. There were also little packages of pinecones, herbs, tobacco, seeds, grass, and a beautiful quartz crystal.

Leonie explained, "I know a bit about the Navajo traditions, and they consider a healing pouch sacred: its contents must be kept secret, so I have added a few for you to choose from. You can decide what goes into it."

Brandon cherished the gift and gave Leonie a hug that lifted her off her feet.

Dillon handed him a leather bag that was heavy and clanked as he took it. He opened it to reveal silver spurs with a beautiful pattern etched onto them.

"WOW! These are amazing! I am going to wear them to the rodeo!"

Dillon told him, "You will fit right in then." He thanked him with a handshake because that was what a man would do. He felt like he was making the passage into manhood today.

Next came his mother's gift; it was a rather large box. It was slightly heavy. Tori had taken the time to decorate it in a Native American material that had stitching and fringe; the colors were vivid blues, reds, black, and white. It was tied with a red ribbon and a bundle of sage was tucked into it. Brandon untied it carefully; opening the lid to the box, he found inside an exquisite pair of boots. They were stressed tan leather; there was a cross pattern adorned by metal studs on the front and back of the quarters, dark piping on the sides and the pull straps. The quarter stitching was a fleur de lis pattern. The instep had a cut-out piece of leather over it with three more crosses cut into it, the largest being at the vamp with a few inlaid studs. The heels were pressed leather, as was the outsole. The spur ridge was sturdy enough to support his new spurs.

Brandon stroked the leather, and it felt supple under his

fingers. "Mom!" he exclaimed, "These are incredible, how could you afford them?"

Tori looked at him with tears in her eyes, "Son, you are worth it a million times over and I am honored for you to have them; you need not worry about how I got them. I love you, Brandon, and they will look good on you."

Brandon put them on and added the spurs. He beamed, and everyone commented on how handsome he looked. I had lit the fire before the gift-giving and suggested we go down to it and make some S'more's.

Brandon blurted, "We can tell ghost stories . . ."

Tori suggested they could find a better topic to discuss on his special day."

"Oh, right, Mom."

"How about we talk about your dreams and future plans, now that you are maturing into manhood."

Everyone agreed they would love to hear about his plans. The fire was blazing and there were blankets for everyone at their chair. They also had a bin with fire roasting sticks for the marshmallows, and one hay bale had a tray on it with the makings for S'more's. Sadie had outdone herself.

After Brandon's tales of his plans for the future, and being stuffed with S'more's, everyone thought it was time for bed. They all felt tired and stuffed! I poured a bucket of water on the fire to douse it. Leonie and Dillon had been next to one another all night long. Brandon had hoped his mom would have been Dillon's date, but he also secretly wished she could be Seth's date more than anyone else's. Dillon and Leonie took their leave together. Tori, Brandon, and I headed inside.

I mentioned, "We can clean up tomorrow as the food has already been put away earlier."

Tori agreed, and they headed to their respective rooms.

CHAPTER EIGHT

I had a dream that night that Tori and I were riding out to the San Cristobal ruins on Cheveyo and Chase. We came to the ruins, tying our horses to the low tree branches. It was nighttime, and the moonlight was shining down on the rock face making the pictographs dance and flicker as if they were coming to life. Tori took my hand and led me towards the cliffs.

She pulled me down in a shaft of moonlight. We fell to the ground with tangled limbs. She was kissing me fiercely. Her tongue darting in and out of my mouth, she traced my lips and gave me little bites. She tore his shirt from my chest and suckled on my nipples, first one and then the other. She trailed soft kisses down my stomach stopping to unbutton my jeans and slid them down my hips only far enough to gain access to my penis. She dived towards me, engulfing me with her mouth; she worked furiously with her tongue, flicking and teasing me. She would swallow me so far down her throat it felt as if I was being devoured. I groaned with pleasure as my passion flared. "Tori," he gasped, "please let me be inside of you." She shot up removing her clothing. The shape of her in the moonlight was intoxicating.

Just as I entered her, I looked into her eyes and I realized it was not Tori, but Anna. I pulled back as if bitten by a snake . . . I awoke from my dream. Drenched in sweat, my body was trembling, and I felt a sense of doom overtaking me.

I looked over at Anna; she was sleeping peacefully. I hoped she could not feel what I had dreamt. I thought about Tori's accusations of Anna being a ghost. *How could she be?* he wondered; *she is so real to me.*

I reached out to stroke her hair, but this time I did not feel her. I jerked my hand back as if I had been bitten once more. How? What? Maybe it was time I faced the facts and listened to what Tori had to say about this crossing over ceremony. He lay there watching Anna as she slept. In my mind I kept thinking about how real she seemed, yet when I had just touched her, she wasn't there. Maybe when she is sleeping, she becomes a hologram or something like that as she is normally in my dreams with me at night. I felt an ache in my heart.

Anna stirred and opened her eyes. She smiled at me, and I

almost forgot that she's not there.

I still had a ranch to run, so I said, "Good morning." I kissed her cheek. This time she felt more solid yet still different from a human felt.

We headed downstairs where Brandon and Tori were already making breakfast. I grabbed my coffee and sat down. Everyone said, "Good morning."

Then there was an awkward silence. I spoke first, "Tori, I am ready to hear what you have to say; Anna, I think you should hear what she has to say also."

Anna looked sheepish as she almost whispered, "Ok."

Tori stuttered and then recovered. She began with an explanation of the gifts she and Brandon shared. "We can 'see' things most others cannot." She looked Anna in the eye, "I know you are not on the earth plane, Anna. I can help you return to the light."

Anna's eyes flashed at that, and she spat out the words, "YOU CANNOT MAKE ME LEAVE!"

Tori calmly reassured her, "No, I cannot force you to leave, but I can assist you in making the transition."

Anna vehemently hissed, "You want Seth for yourself, and you are trying to get rid of me!"

At this time, Brandon interjected, "I also want to help you cross over."

Anna glared, "Of course, you do, and then you could have

the father you never had."

Tori was visibly upset by the attack on her son but remained calm, "Anna, Brandon just wants to help you as do I."

"It is because of what's in it for you, both of you!" She looked at me, spitting the words at him as well. "And you, YOU want Tori! That is why you want to get rid of me. You are all conspiring against me!"

I ground my teeth to remain calm as I responded, "Anna, darlin,' we want what is best for you. If you want, we can go to see your father, and he will tell you that he wants the same thing for you."

Anna became pensive for a moment; she slit her eyes and looked back at Tori. Tori dared not say a word, so she continued to gaze into Anna's eyes imploring her to listen. Anna finally broke the silence, "I will listen to what you have to say, but in no way does this mean I have agreed to leave."

"Fair enough," replied Tori, "I was trained by my grandmother in the ways of the medicine woman. Brandon and I have the gift of 'seeing' and we both thought you were real." Continuing with the reason behind that, she explained, "You were drawing energy from all of the things around you, animate and inanimate objects alike."

She added, "It is one of the reasons your father was unable to maintain his sanity. The difference between a spirit and a ghost or trapped soul is one has crossed into the light but the other missed the opportunity and has become stuck here."

Anna asked, "Please clarify that."

"A ghost or trapped soul is a person who has left their body becoming trapped in the ether, not entering the light. They do not exist on the material plane either. Many times, they do not realize they have passed on from this life. A spirit has entered the light and can come and go on the earth plane, assisting their loved ones without drawing energy from them as they are complete in the light. They become the highest form of love, the highest vibration; they are like angels or light beings. Being of the light, they can travel as light does."

Anna retorted, "Okay. What happens when and IF I allow this ceremony to take place?"

Tori explained, "Brandon and I will prepare by fasting and then entering a sweat lodge so we may journey into the Spirit world. When we are cleansed and the vision is clearly shown to us, we will know what to do.

"We will go to the place where you, Anna, had passed from your body, the bridge out on U.S. 285 over Galisteo Creek. We call your soul to us using white sage and prayer. I will ask that a white light vortex is opened for you to enter through; so, you may go into the light. We will watch you pass through that vortex, normally accompanied by loved ones that have previously passed."

Tori confided, "Your mother is willing to help us."

Anna asked, "You have spoken to my mother?"

Tori confirmed, "Yes, I have asked for her help."

Anna asked, "After I go. Can I come back here right away?"

"I do not know how it works exactly, but I know that it is a place of great love and comfort."

Anna looked at me, "I want to see my father, and then I will let you know what decision I have chosen." Anna asked, "Do you want me to go?"

Through a choked voice, I affirmed, "I love you, and I want you to be happy." Tears began to fall from my eyes as I buried my face in my hands to hide them.

Anna excused herself. The others sat in silence for a moment. Tori looked at me, "Seth, I am so sorry for what you are experiencing right now, but in time things will get better."

She was unprepared for my reaction. I stood up knocking my chair to the ground. I cursed, "Damn you! Before you came here, we had a perfect life; this is your fault!" Cursing under his breath, I strode from the room

Tori sat there stunned as a tear rolled down her cheek. Brandon pleaded with her not to cry. "Mom, it is okay, please don't cry. He will see it is for the best. It will be okay."

"I just want to help them."

"Mom, I know you do; they will understand someday." He

held her close as she let go of her sorrow.

Anna arrived at her father's side. She implored, "Daddy, do you really want me to leave?"

He demanded to know what she was talking about, "Why would you say that princess?"

She told the story of Tori's plan to help her cross into the light. He said, "My sweet princess, I want you to be happy, and if you cross into the light, as your mother has, you can see me any time without having to be stuck here. You will be free, like the angel that you are."

Looking up at him, she knelt by his side. She complied, "If that is what you wish daddy, I will go. I love you so much."

"Princess, I love you too, with all of my heart."

"I am going to return to the ranch and tell Tori to prepare for the ceremony. Bye, Daddy, I shall always love you."

When she appeared to Tori, she felt relieved. She was becoming angry and restless in this place of nothingness. She told Tori, "I have made a decision."

Tori feared the worst.

Anna asserted, "I am ready to enter the light now."

Tori was surprised that Anna wanted to go to the light. Tori assured her, "Brandon and I will go home to the rez and prepare right away." They gathered their things and got into the Jeep.

Anna asked them, "Where is Seth?"

Brandon answered her, "He was quite angry with my mother and has gone to the barn."

As they pulled away, Anna went to the barn. Seth was nowhere to be seen. Chase was gone, too. Anna suspected he was up on the north ridge. She had no reason to pretend to walk there anymore and she appeared on the ridge almost immediately. Sure enough, Seth was there. Chase was ground tied near him. He was squatting with his face in his hands. Anna not only heard his sobs but also saw the way his body shook from them. Anna's presence startled Chase, and he shied.

I looked up, jumping to my feet. I caught the reins in one hand. "Anna," was all I could manage to say.

Anna looked at him with a new respect. She could see the love he had for her. How did she ever doubt him? "Seth, I just spoke with Daddy." I continued to stare at her. She went on, "I have decided to go into the light and join my momma."

I fell to my knees and begged, "Please Anna, please don't leave me . . . Anna, I love you!"

"Seth, I now know this is the best thing for me, so do not worry. I will be your guardian angel always and forever."

Looking up, I gushed, "Oh, Anna."

"Let's go back to the house and spend some quality time together before I go." I took Chase and followed her to the barn.

Later when we were settled in the den, she told me, "I wish to read some meditations to you, to help with the grieving." I sat on the sofa. She began:

"Birth is not the beginning and death is not the end (Chuang-Tsu).

Let life be beautiful like the summer and death like the autumn leaves (Tagore).

If you would indeed behold the spirit of death, open your heart wide into the body of life. For life and death are one, even as the river and the sea are one (Kahlil Gibran).

I often think that people we have loved and who have loved us . . . become a part of us and we carry them around all of the time-whether we see them or not. And in some ways we are a sum total of those who have loved us and those we have given ourselves to (Anonymous)."

I looked at her and told her, "I love you so much Anna, and what you just read was not only a comfort to me but beautiful also."

"I am scared to leave, but I know in my heart it is the right thing to do. I want to see my mother again," she confided.

I said, "Anna, I will miss you."

"I will always be there in your heart. We are bound together by our heartstrings, forever and ever."

Tori and Brandon drove to the Four Corners Rez in Farmington. They arrived just before dark set in. Tori's Uncle, Niyol, opened the door, "Niece, it is so good to see you and nephew as well."

They explained the situation to their Uncle. He said, "We will begin by starting the fast tonight. In the morning I will make the sand paintings and prepare the sweat lodge. We must pray together. Niyol began, "Treat the earth and all that dwell thereon with respect, remain close to the Great Spirit, show great respect for your fellow beings, work together for the benefit of all humankind, give assistance and kindness wherever needed, do what you know to be right, look after the well-being of mind and body, dedicate a share of your efforts to the greater good, be truthful and honest at all times, and take full responsibility for your actions."

He ended with "Oh Great Spirit, hear our prayers."

In unison, Brandon and Tori chanted, "A'ho."

"We must now sit in the Hogan for the night asking for guidance from our creator. The Great Spirit will show us the way to help our sister enter the Spirit world. Let us put on our ceremonial clothes."

When they were done in preparing, he led them to the Hogan behind his house next to the sweat lodge. He lifted the door flap as he said a prayer for guidance. They entered from the East, each placed something on the sacred alter before entering.

Once inside, they took seats cross-legged in a circle. There was a circle of sage on the floor with a sacred pipe in the center of the circle. Uncle picked up the peace pipe and they smoked. He then handed rattles to each of them and picked up his drum. As they played in rhythm he began to chant:

"Chanah naadleet dii iliigo doolado ni ei shika aalwod doolado kwii dah she' iina kwii ha niih."

They entered a trance-like state and sat in the Hogan until sunset of the following day.

Each one had seen a vision of what they must do. Niyol reminded them what the sweat lodge symbolizes.

"The symbolism of the steam and the structure of the sweat lodge represents the womb, life's starting place. It has developed in the form of a ceremony, working respectfully with the essential elements—water, fire, air or wind, and earth—to create a powerful purification on all levels. It provides the possibility of expansion that allows us to directly connect with the Great Spirit.

"Silence, prayer, and tribal music will support us on the journey. There will be four rounds after the dusting off ceremony, which will each represent one of the four directions. Pay particular attention to the East, birth, and the West, death, for we must help Anna be reborn through the door of the underworld, death, to enter the heavens and join with our Creator."

Uncle led them from the Hogan to the sweat lodge where they would do a dusting off round with seven stones. He had a helper prepare the fire and heat the stones while they had been praying, asking for a vision. They blew the conch shell to the four directions, to the Mother Earth, and to the Father. The helper began putting the stones into the lodge one at a time repeating "A'ho" with each stone that was placed in the center of the lodge. He added the herbs, sage, cedar, and tobacco.

They entered the lodge from the East, taking seats on the earthen floor, and Uncle poured water over the stones. "We honor the four elements, fire, water, earth, and wind."

Tori and Brandon said, "A'ho."

They began to inhale the herbs cleansing their bodies, minds, souls, and spirits. The door was opened two more times to honor the directions of South and North. When they could take no more, Uncle blew the conch shell. The door flap was opened, and they left from the West. At this time, they were to break the fast by drinking water and eating corn, berries, and a nut mixture.

Uncle closed with a prayer to the Great Spirit:

"Oh, Great Spirit, whose voice I hear in the wind, whose breath gives life to the entire world. Hear me; I need your strength and wisdom. Let me walk in beauty, make my eyes ever behold the red and purple sunset. Make my hands respect the things you have made and my ears sharp to hear your voice. Make me wise so I may understand the things you have taught my people. Help me to remain calm and strong in the face of all that comes towards me. Let me learn the lessons you have hidden in every leaf and rock. Help me seek pure thoughts and act with the intention of helping others. Help me find compassion without empathy overwhelming me. I seek strength, not to be greater than my brother, but to fight my greatest enemy; myself. Make me always ready to come to you with clean hands and straight eyes. So, when life fades, as the fading sunset, my spirit may come to you without shame. A'ho."

Tori and Brandon hugged Niyol. He asked, "Was your vision clear?"

Tori said, "I was shown the way to lead the ceremony. I was also shown that I must mix the old ways of our people with the new age ways to help my friend find her way home."

Brandon answered, "I was told to say a prayer and use the drum during the ceremony."

CHAPTER NINE

I awoke from my dream with a smile on my face Last night, Anna was like a seductress. She strode across the room dressed in heels and a slinky see-through nightie; she pushed me to the bed and leaned over him, kissing me firmly on my lips, as she pulled away she took my bottom lip between her teeth and bit me ever so gently before releasing my lip. She did a sensuous dance as she removed my clothing. Crawling across the floor, she turned onto her back with her legs in the air and wiggled around before rolling to her side and pushing herself up as she flung her hair back. I was rock hard; I thought I may rupture from my need to penetrate her. She practically pounced on top of him catching him off guard; she slid on top of me and began to ride me in a circular motion. I thrust into her with such force I thought she may break, but she met me thrust for thrust. She leaned down and nibbled on my ear, whispering to me as she swirled on top of me.

I could no longer restrain myself and rolled over so that Anna was on her back; I spread my legs and entered her with a growl as she whimpered. She dug her nails into my hips and pulled me into her as if she could not get enough of me. As she arched her back, I heaved and pushed into her harder. We both began to tremble and reached climax at the same moment. Lying spent on the bed, gasping, I knew that this was my parting gift.

Tori called me, "We have had our visions, and we are preparing to come later in the day."

She asked, "Is Anna ready to go?"

He looked at Anna and asked her the question. She affirmed, "I am."

Tori told him, "Okay then, we will see you soon. I will text when we are headed your way."

I ended the call and looked at Anna. I said, "I guess this is it."

Anna told him again, "I will always be here with you. Love must live on in the heart; at least, that is what Tori said."

"I wish we had more time."

"Cherish what we were given and be grateful for it. I know I am."

Tori and Brandon parked near the house. They went in to

get me and told Anna to meet them at the bridge. I was in a foul mood. I had just walked in from the barn and told them, "I need to change my clothes before we leave." Tori noticed my tone was short and gruff.

Brandon noticed the tension between his mom and me. He said, "Don't worry, Mom, it will be okay once he realizes this is what's best for Anna."

When she answered, it was little more than a whisper saying, "I know." I returned and we headed to the Jeep. I wanted to sit in the back seat. No one wanted to argue with me. They set off for the bridge.

The drive was a tense hour and a half long. Most of it was done in silence. When we reached the bridge, Anna was there waiting. She did not look like the Anna we knew. I gasped audibly. Anna's skin had patches of discoloring, red and grey where hypostasis and lividity had set in. She looked bluish, and her eyes and hair were brown.

"Oh my God, Anna!" I exclaimed.

"Please calm down," Tori continued. "These are the physiological changes that had occurred at the time of her passing. A ghost will normally maintain the look they had upon their death, as well as wearing the same clothing. In Anna's case, she had developed ways to transform herself by drawing power from those around her, both animate and inanimate objects. She had what is called obsession with her father, which created him to appear as if he had lost his sanity. Symptoms begin with insomnia, loss of appetite, low energy, and exhaustion, and end up with the person becoming depressed.

"In your case, Seth, she took possession; this may occur when a person is stressed from lack of money, loss of a loved one, or drug use. The electromagnetic field will also disrupt appliances and other electronic devices such as static on a cellular phone. Now that Anna has agreed to cross over the physical effects will lessen, and with energy healing sessions her father and you should recover completely. It is very important to repair the chakras . . ."

I glared at Tori, "I do not want you to touch me; you have done enough damage in my life."

Tori felt as if she had been slapped but replied as calm as possible, "If not me, then someone else, as it is very important to heal from this ordeal."

Anna said to me, "I release you, please get help to heal, Seth."

My body shuddering, I looked at Anna, teared up, and begged her to stay.

She told him, "It is best for me and everyone around me if I go; if you search your heart, you will know it is true. Listen to Tori; she is wise in the ways of the Spirit. My mother told me to listen to her and I did; now I know the truth."

He cried, "I know that, but it does not stop the pain I feel."

Tori told Brandon and Anna, "We must begin."

Brandon lit the sage, and they held a smudging ceremony. Next, Tori poured sea salt in a large circle around them for protection from malevolent forces. Brandon got out his shaman drum; it was beautiful with a yin-yang of two horses on the front in black and white. There were decorated feathers and beads hanging from the drumstick. He began to beat the drum slowly and rhythmically.

Tori began by reading the prayer of beauty:

"In beauty I walk

With beauty before me I walk

With beauty behind me I walk

With beauty above me I walk

With beauty around me I walk

It has become beauty again

It has become beauty again

It has become beauty again

It has become beauty again"

Then she began to chant it in her Navajo language:

"Hózhóogo naasháa doo

Shitsijí' hózhóogo naasháa doo

Shikéédéé hózhóogo naasháa doo

Shideigi hózhóogo naasháa doo

T'áá altso shinaagóó hózhóogo naasháa doo

Hózhó náhásdlíí'

Hózhó náhásdlíí'

Hózhó náhásdlíí'

Hózhó náhásdlíí'"

Brandon took over the chant as Tori focused on Anna, "Anna, are you ready to cross over?"

Anna replied, "I am."

Tori made some movements with her hands in a spiral motion while asking a blessing from Creator, Great Spirit. She looked asked her, "Can you now see the light?"

Anna replied, "It is there, but faint."

Tori called upon Anna's mother Rose, who appeared immediately, walking over to her daughter and taking her hand. She gently led her to the source of light. When they arrived at the tunnel, they turned, Anna was glowing, now looking her radiant self. "Goodbye," they imparted these words, "Remember that love is the most important thing on earth and always follow your heart." They turned and were engulfed by the bright light so bright that those on the ground had to shield their eyes.

Brandon stopped drumming and intoned a prayer:

"Final Vision

Life is the flash of a firefly in the night.

It is the breath of the buffalo in the winter.

It is the little shadow which runs across the grass

and loses itself in the sunset. -Crowfoot (Blackfoot)"

Tori closed with the Walking in Beauty blessing, the Navajo
way:

"Today I will walk out, today everything unnecessary will leave me,

I will be as I was before, I will have a cool breeze over my body.

I will have a light body, I will be happy forever,

nothing will hinder me.

I walk with beauty before me. I walk with beauty behind me.

I walk with beauty below me. I walk with beauty above me.

I walk with beauty around me. My words will be beautiful.

In beauty all day long may I walk.

Through the returning seasons, may I walk.

On the trail marked with pollen may I walk.

With dew about my feet, may I walk.

With beauty before me may I walk.

With beauty behind me may I walk.

With beauty below me may I walk.

With beauty above me may I walk.

With beauty all around me may I walk.

In old age wandering on a trail of beauty, lively, may I walk.

In old age wandering on a trail of beauty, living again, may I walk.

My words will be beautiful."

Everyone felt spent. Tori and Brandon laid crystals, sage, and rose petals at the place of the accident, saying their goodbyes. They looked to me and asked me, "Would you like to leave something?" I went to the place and laid down the necklace he had given Anna. Beside it, I dug a small hole and then placed it inside, burying it so it would remain safely in this spot. I arose with dirt on my hands. Brushing them on my jeans, I strode to the car. The ride home was just as tense and awkward as before.

I got out of the car without a word. Tori did not dare speak to me. Brandon asked, "Should I come to work tomorrow?"

Walking away, I growled, "No!" They heard the door slam behind me as I entered the house. Tori felt lost and helpless.

Brandon told her, "I have to go to the barn and get Cheveyo." She drove him back to the barn and helped him gather his things, putting what he could not take on horseback into the car. As Brandon led Cheveyo from the barn the other horses pawed and whinnied in their stalls. Brandon mounted with a heavy heart.

Tori said, "I will see you at home." As Tori drove home, she thought about a poem by Goethe: "The thought of death leaves me in perfect peace, for I have a firm conviction that our spirit is a being of indestructible nature; it works on from eternity to eternity; it is like the sun, which though it seems to set to our mortal eyes, does not really set, but shines on perpetually."

I stared at the car as Tori pulled out of the driveway. I saw Brandon riding towards the ridge. I would miss the boy, but I could not bear to think about Tori's betrayal and seeing Ma'ii would just be a reminder of that.

Maybe a ride would do me good. I went to the barn and saddled Chase. At the last minute I decided to pony George along. A saying by June Singer got stuck in my head, and I thought of how much it reminded him of Anna. "Awareness of approach to death can be a beautiful thing, a frame into which we can put the work of art that is our life, our personal masterpiece." I went to the north ridge and secured the horses. I lay on a boulder to stare at the sky. I drifted off to sleep.

Brandon rode towards home and repeated a prayer that he loved by Evelyn Eaton; *"Great Spirit, when we face the sunset, when we come singing the last song, may it be without shame, singing it is finished in beauty, it is finished in beauty!"* He thought that it was fitting as Anna's crossing over ceremony was a beautiful rite of passage. He thought how lucky he was that he was raised to respect death as a part of life. His people had a great understanding of life, death, and the spirit world. Those raised in the Whiteman's world did not usually have that luxury.

My brother Sandoval called me to no avail. He decided after the tenth time to leave a message. "Seth, its Sandoval. I have your financial reports finished and a cost analysis also. It seems that the ranch will be an excellent investment for you. At this time, I am sorry I cannot come on board. We found out that Alpina and I are going to have a little brother or a little sister for Angeline! We are pretty excited and, after a long discussion, thought it best to not make any new investments at this time. The cost of raising a child is not cheap! Hope this finds you well, Alpina, Angeline, and I send our love."

Tori called Leonie, "Can I come over for tea?"

Leonie answered, "Sure if you come right now, as later I have a date."

"I am happy for you, Leonie. Who is the lucky guy?"

"Well . . . it is Dillon. He and I hit it off, and we want to explore things a bit further."

"Wow," exclaimed Tori. "That is great! I will be there in about ten minutes."

When Tori arrived, she found Leonie covered in paint with her hair in a messy bun. "What on earth have you been up to?"

Leonie told her, "I felt my creative juices flowing and had to paint something." She led Tori over to an easel where there was a large canvas propped upon it. There was an incredible painting of elephants with a reddish background and the words of a Kahlil Gibran poem behind the image in gold. It said, "If you would behold the spirit of death, open your heart wide into the body of life. For life and death are one, even as the river and sea are one."

Tori told her, "This is prophetic as I have just completed a crossing over ceremony."

Leonie asked, "Anyone I know?"

Tori told her, "As a matter of fact, you do. It was Anna, as in Seth's Anna, the Anna I grew up with."

Astonished, Leonie said, "This is a story I must hear. Why have you kept this from me?"

Tori explained, "Anna was a powerful ghost that appeared real to me and to Brandon. Also, to her own father and Seth." She continued, "Remember that you did not get to meet her as she had a headache the night of the party? Well, that was her excuse to stay away from others that she thought could not see her. To keep Seth from realizing he was in love with a ghost.

"She was hanging around one day though, and Brandon and I could see her; once she realized this, she played us into believing she was alive. She did seem real. I did some research and some ghosts can acquire supernatural powers. Anna became one of those powerful beings.

"It was Brandon who figured it out first as he saw her standing by her father's side when he and Seth went to visit him to ask about buying the ranch."

Leonie said, "Well, I'll be!"

"Seth is angry with me for what he called 'sending Anna away.' I am heartbroken because I have developed feelings for him." A tear traced down her cheek.

Leonie assured her, "Men are stubborn, never wanting to appear weak to us. Just give him time, Tori. He will come around; he will eventually see the light!"

Tori replied, "Seeing the light is what started this!" They giggled at the pun.

Tori asked all about Dillon and what they had planned

tonight. Leonie said, "He wants me to be dressed in cowgirl garb. We are going to the stable to take a sunset ride, and then we will retire to his teepee."

"His WHAT?"

"I guess he lives in a teepee at the stables. He said it sits on the top of a hill, and he can keep an eye on the whole operation from up there. He cooks on a campfire every day!"

"Well, I think I will start calling you Pocahontas from now on," she laughed.

Leonie made them some wonderful flower and sage tea. She served it with lemon lavender biscuits. Tori almost inhaled her biscuit as she had not eaten much over the last few days due to the ceremony.

Leonie offered to cook for her.

"Oh no, I have to get home to Brandon as he helped me, and he will be starving, too. Besides, you have to get ready for your date!"

Leonie saw her friend to the door and waved as she drove away. Now she had to take a goddess shower and prepare for tonight!

Brandon got home just minutes after Tori went inside the house. She had begun making tacos for them. He came in and told her, "Mom, I am famished, and I could eat ten tacos!"

Tori replied, "I wouldn't doubt it." She served him five to

start, "I will make more if your stomach is indeed bigger than your eyes."

Next, she asked him, "Do want to talk about what has happened today and about Seth's reaction to it?"

"I was hurt by his rejection, but I will continue to send him positive energy and prayers."

Tori looked at him with admiration; she felt she was raising him right. Well, that and the help of her tribe. The saying "it takes a village" could not be truer. The elders were an integral part of bringing up the youth of her tribe.

Dillon was prepping for his date with Leonie. He could not get over how cute she was. Slightly plump, she was glowing. Her eyes twinkled, and her mass of curls intrigued him. Oh, how he wanted to tangle his hands in them. He put on his best button-down and newly starched Wranglers; he even dabbed on a bit of cologne. He donned his cowboy hat and headed for his pickup. He drove a Dodge dooly. He loved the power behind its Triton V-10 Engine. Most people in these parts drove a diesel truck, but he liked the power his truck had. He swore it could move a house if it had to. Too bad Ford quit making them. He thought to himself, *Ole' Bessy is a collector's item.* He pulled up to Leonie's house and honked. She looked out and motioned him in.

She watched him, all limbs, and length. As he got out of the truck. He was tall and sturdy, but not too muscular. He had a strong nose, with blue-green eyes that lit up like a little boy when he laughed. His golden-brown hair was wavy, although it was normally under that darn hat. Leonie chuckled, *Tonight I am gonna give him a reason to take his hat off.*

She gave him a hug and a peck on the cheek when he came in. She said just give me a minute to take care of the dogs and leave a note for the guests, and then we can head out.

The road to the stable was dusty, so Dillon turned on the air and rolled up the windows. Leonie told him, "I am not a sissy; you can roll the windows back down."

He said, "I know, but ya' look so pretty; I didn't want ya to get all dirty." He told her, "I will let you ride my horse Pearl, and I will ride my new horse, a three-year-old in training. I named her Sapphire.

"I cannot wait to meet them," she said. When they got to the corral, Leonie walked over and gently blew up the horses' nostrils.

He asked her, "How do you know how horses greet one another?"

She explained, "In my 'other life,' I raised horses and learned the ways of the horse whisperer Buck Brannaman."

Dillon was quite impressed by this fact. He said, "Pearl is gonna love you." They saddled up and set out on the trail through the park just as the sun became a huge orange disk on the horizon. Soon the sky would be like a watercolor painted by God's paintbrush. *So romantic*, thought Leonie.

As I slept on the boulder, I had a new kind of dream. Anna came to me again, but this time she was golden and shining brightly, almost as if she had a halo above her. She told me, "The ethereal plane is unlike anything on earth, it vibrates love, and it is love." She explained, "There is no jealousy here, no malice, just love. God is Love and Love is God."

She reached out her hand to touch him; it was like a feather had landed on his heart. With her touch, he could actually feel the love she spoke of. She said, "I must be in a transitory place for a while, but after that, I will be able to watch over you and Daddy." She gently whispered in my ear, "Forgiveness is the key to opening your heart so you may receive the love. Never forget that."

With that, she vanished. I awoke with a start. Maybe I was too hard on Tori and Brandon, but I still wasn't ready to forgive them. Maybe Tori used her magic to send me this dream . . . after today anything was possible as far as I was concerned.

Dillon and Leonie had just returned from their ride, it had been perfect, with amazing views. After they untacked, watered and brushed down the horses, Dillon led her to his teepee. He asked her to have a seat in the dining room. Leonie had to ask, "Where would that be located?"

He waved his arm to a picnic table beside the fire pit. She said, "Oh, I see what a lovely dining room it is; you have decorated it splendidly." He loved her sense of humor and how she could just go with the flow. He stoked the fire and set to work, preparing a meal for them on top of the grate. He even had wine chilling in an ice bucket on the table, AND cloth napkins with the cutest little horse head napkin rings, although they were eating on paper plates, she loved it!

Tori spent a restless night and decided to get out of bed

early instead of lying there, fretting over things she had no control over. When she walked into the kitchen, she found Brandon preparing breakfast. She asked him what he was doing up so early. He said, "I could not sleep, and I want to go to work with you today. Maybe I can be your assistant."

"I would love the company."

CHAPTER TEN

Leonie woke up and realized she was naked on a buffalo skin, in a teepee, and there was no other place she would rather be.

But she had guests at her B & B, meaning bed AND breakfast, she better hightail it home. Dillon rolled over and said, "Leavin' so soon?"

She explained, "I have to tend to my guests. What kind of B & B doesn't serve breakfast?"

He suggested, "The just B kind."

She had to laugh but still grabbed her clothes and told him, "Please take me home." They made it just as the guests were coming downstairs. She pretended that she was just out in the hen house gathering eggs, but her guests weren't fooled. They teased her with an "Oooh la la . . . had a hot date, huh?"

She blushed as she asked, "Would you prefer tea or coffee?"

Dillon texted her that he would love to see her again soon, adding an XO.

He headed over to see Seth. He had some great ideas for the ranch, and Seth was not answering his phone.

Dillon drove straight back to the barn, he saw me tending to the horses. He hopped out of his truck and went over to help me, as they fed the animals, he told me about his ideas.

He said, "I was thinking we could offer sunset rides, you certainly have the space to add horses. Chuck-wagon dinners and even paying to attend a mini-cattle drive would bring in money." He told me he was going to ask Tori and Brandon if they could run horseback tours to the San Cristobal ruins. He said, "We could even host weddings here, so with the hay, cattle, and tourism, this place would stay afloat."

I looked at him and said, "I thought you were the silent partner."

"Well, gee Seth, that is not the answer I was hoping for; I thought there might be a little more excitement on your part. What's eatin' you anyway?"

"Remember that situation I mentioned before the party? Well, that is what's eatin' me."

Dillon Inquired, "How so?"

I hung my head and told him the whole story from start to

end.

"Wow Seth, I find it hard to believe, but I am keeping an open mind."

"The worst part is now I have no reason to buy the ranch."

"Seth, I think you know better than that. You don't wanna' end up like ole' man Ames, do ya? Locked away in an institution?"

I felt defeated right now, but I said, "No, I sure don't, but maybe that would be better than being here in pain; at least, they could drug me there."

"Come on," Dillon said, "That is a piss poor attitude if I ever heard one."

"I was on the ridge most of the night, and I couldn't help but think I might be better off joining Anna."

Dillon looked disgusted, "Man! Grow a backbone; I have never before known you to be so spineless. While you're at it, grow a pair as well!"

"Lay off it, okay!"

Dillon noticed he did not see Ma'ii and asked, "Where is Ma'ii?"

I retorted, "I told him he was no longer needed and asked Tori to stay away too."

Dillon felt sad for him and thought nothing he was saying seems to snap me outta this stupor I was in. He said, "Ya know, I guess I would not want to have a partner that is feelin' sorry for himself anyway. I guess I will be on my way. If ya need anything, call me."

I did not even bother waving goodbye.

Sadie was in the house cooking and wondering what in tarnation was going on around here. She was alone. I never showed up for his "fuel" as I called it, and that boy with an appetite of a Sasquatch was also absent. She kept about her business, and soon I came in. She said, "You look a fright, Mr. Seth. Ya' want some coffee or vittles?"

"Just coffee, please."

She got it for him and began putting away the food.

"I would be glad to lend an ear if ya need one."

I thought about it, but then remembered Sadie loved to gossip, and this was one story I did not want floatin' around town. Sipping my coffee, I said, "It's personal, but thank."

After a while, Sadie said, "Your face has woman troubles written all over it. I am gonna' bend your ear with a bit of unsolicited advice."

I thought here it comes . . . Sadie began, "I have seen how you and that woman Tori look at one another, and that boy, well, he adores you. I think that unrequited love is the worst kind of love. I mean if ya ask me, even though ya didn't."

I thought to himself, *Was it that obvious*? Could she really see my attraction to Tori, and how did I not see Tori's attraction to me. Probably it was because I was always feeling guilty about betraying Anna with my thoughts. "Thank you, Sadie, for your advice," I informed her, "I have to make a trip into Albuquerque. You can have the day off."

She asked, "With pay?"

"Of course," I replied.

I cleaned up and set off for the Sage Rehabilitation & Care Center in Albuquerque. I arrived at supper time. The nurse led me to the dining room. The food made me have second thoughts about wantin' to be institutionalized. I sat down next to Silas.

Silas asked, "What can I do for ya, boy?"

"Do you know that Anna has been crossed over by Tori and Brandon?"

"I do, son. I helped her make the decision. She is now with her momma and they are both happy," Silas added. "Tori will be working with me so I can heal; she will be seeing me once a week. We have the first session planned for Friday evening."

I was surprised. "Well, did you know Anna and I had been living together for over a year at the ranch?"

"Anna spoke about that from time to time."

I thought this conversation is like pullin' teeth. I explained, "I loved Anna, I still do, and I am upset at Tori for taking her away."

"Boy, you should be happy she went to that place of Love, PURE LOVE. She will always be in your heart. Nothing lasts forever. You got to experience love, which is more than most get in their lifetime. Think about what kind of love it was though; was it a selfish love or a selfless, giving love?"

That last comment hit me in the solar plexus as if I had taken a blow. Thinking back, I would have to say it was selfish. I loved the sex, the nights where Anna and I met in the dream world; the place where I felt ecstasy. All of my dreams came flooding back to him, not just of Anna, but of Tori and Brandon, too. I thanked him for his wisdom. I said, "You have shown me something I was too blind to see. I have a second chance at love . . . selfless love." I hugged the old man, startling him.

Silas said, "Glad I could be of service young buck." I got up to leave promising to visit again. I had one stop to make first.

I decided to go directly to Tori; I thought he would find her at the ruins. When I arrived, she was just breaking for lunch. All of the tourists were seated in the shade at picnic tables, and she and Brandon were passing out the boxed lunches. Great, they were both here. I stepped up behind Tori and said, "Excuse me, Ma'am."

She turned as she said, "What can I help you with?"

Her face looked shocked as she saw it was I, and not a client behind her. "Seth?" she questioned, "what are you doing here? I am working."

I made a sweeping gesture with his arm, "I am sure these fine people won't mind an interruption."

Everyone agreed they wouldn't mind. I asked Brandon to come near and whispered in his ear. Brandon grinned and shook his head. I bent down on one knee; I pulled a small bag out of his pocket and produced a ring. It was exquisite; it was handcrafted Silver with a Herkimer diamond and Turquoise stones. I took Tori's hand in mine as I gazed into her eyes, I asked her, "Would you be my wife and partner for life?"

For a moment Tori could not speak; she could not breathe! At last, she answered, "Yes! Yes, I will be your wife and partner for life!" I picked her up and twirled her around as everyone applauded us. I thanked everyone for their hospitality and told her and Brandon to come by the ranch on their way home.

I called Dillon on my way home and asked if he and Leonie could head over to the ranch. I apologized for behaving like a jerk the last couple of days, but told him, "Wise words from an old man helped me to see the light and change my ways." I added, "I have a big surprise."

Dillon could not believe the change in me. He called Leonie and asked her to come on over so they could head to the ranch together.

She said, "Well, I will have to meet you there as I need to take care of my guests first."

Dillon said, "No problem sugar, I will see you there."

I checked my messages. I heard the one from Sandoval. I rang him back. Sandoval answered on the second ring. I told my brother, "I am glad you are alive and well, Seth."

"Congratulations on the baby!" I told him and then shared his own good news, "I just got engaged, Bro."

"Wow, that is wonderful news; the cowboy is settling down, huh?"

"Yes, he is, and she has a teenage son. I am going to have an instant family!" I remembered to thank him for his work on the financials. I said, "I have found a silent partner that is not so silent," and they laughed. I also shared the new plan to bring in income.

Sandoval said, "This makes the investment even better. I can make the changes and send over the plan via fax, so you can share it with your partner."

I thanked him and hung up. He called Sadie and asked her for an emergency dinner. She at first gave me a piece of her mind, but after I explained why I needed her, she said, "I will head right out!" I had one more call to make. I called the preacher!

I raced home and set up a makeshift archway on the ridge. I did my best to decorate it with wildflowers. I even made a small bouquet for Tori. I got the horses ready in the barn so that they could be led up to the ridge for the photos afterward. I knew Leonie was artistic and would leave those to her. *Now to get myself cleaned up.* I jumped in the shower, and when I emerged all shiny and new, I could smell a feast being prepared downstairs. I went down to the kitchen and thanked Sadie in person, even givin' her a playful pat on the bottom.

She just said, "Lordy, what has gotten into you?"

"Well, first, some wise people talked some sense into me! Next, we are going to be a working Ranch!" I told her about the plan to have chuck-wagon dinners, mini cattle drives, tours, and weddings at the ranch and asked her to sign on as the official vittles maker.

She smiled from ear to ear, "I will accept the position."

I heard a car pull in; it was Dillon, next came Leonie. He yelled out the window to Leonie. "I picked up a couple of dresses for you and Tori. I guessed the sizes, can you come up and check them out?"

She ran upstairs, and a few moments later came down in hers, "Tori's is gorgeous, it will fit her fine." They were native leather decorated with beads. Leonie asked, "Do I get to keep mine?"

"No, sorry, I have to return them tomorrow."

I grinned, "I am just pullin' your leg." I heard another car pull in, this time it was Tori and Brandon. I went out to meet them.

Tori noticed Dillon and Leonie's vehicles in the drive. She said, "Are you having a party?"

I said, "No, WE are havin' a party; now go get ready missy!"

Leonie took her upstairs and helped her into her dress. When they came down, everyone exclaimed how beautiful the girls were. I said, "Time to head to the barn." I handed Leonie his camera and we collected the horses. When we got to the top of the ridge, Tori saw the arch and a local minister standing by it.

"Seth? What is this?"

I said with a wink, "It looks like a weddin'! I did not want to waste one more minute without you by my side, so this is our wedding!"

Tori thought this was the most romantic thing she had ever experienced. I handed her the small bouquet of wildflowers; she looked at me and exclaimed, "I love redneck roses!"

Everyone took their places: Brandon, the best man; Dillon, the horse handler; and Leonie, the maid of honor cum photographer.

The minister began with the usual, and after he did his part, I said I wanted to read my vows to her, "Well, actually a poem, I can't take the credit." Everyone laughed.

"We are the night ocean filled with glints of light. We are the space between the fish and the moon. While we sit here together. Sometimes afraid of reunion, sometimes afraid of separation. You and I, so fond of the notion of a you and an I, should live as though we'd never heard those pronouns." (Rumi)

"We shall now live as one Catori, I love you," I added. "Well, we shall live as two because I love Brandon too!" He received more giggles for his humor.

As Tori gazed at him with love, a tear rolled down her cheek, when she leaned in for the "you may kiss the bride" part, she saw an apparition over my shoulder near the trees. She recognized it at once as Anna; then she heard in her head and with her heart, "You both have my blessing." She silently thanked her. Anna added, "After all, there is no jealousy in heaven, only love."

I looked at Tori and said, "I swear I just heard Anna give us her blessing."

"She did, Seth. She is finally at peace," she then kissed her man.

Tori and I turned around as the minister said, "I now present Mr. and Mrs. Anderson!"

Tori threw her bouquet, and Leonie caught it.

I winked at Dillon, "I think you might be our first customer for a ranch-style wedding!"

THE END

Made in the USA
Monee, IL
21 April 2020

26691763R00125